A TRUTHFUL INJUSTICE

Recent Titles by Jeffrey Ashford from Severn House

THE COST OF INNOCENCE
AN HONEST BETRAYAL
LOOKING-GLASS JUSTICE
MURDER WILL OUT
A TRUTHFUL INJUSTICE
A WEB OF CIRCUMSTANCES

Writing as Roderic Jeffries

DEFINITELY DECEASED
SEEING IS DECEIVING

A TRUTHFUL
INJUSTICE

Jeffrey Ashford

This first world edition published in Great Britain 2002 by
SEVERN HOUSE PUBLISHERS LTD of
9–15 High Street, Sutton, Surrey SM1 1DF.
This first world edition published in the USA 2002 by
SEVERN HOUSE PUBLISHERS INC of
595 Madison Avenue, New York, N.Y. 10022.

British Library Cataloguing in Publication Data

Ashford, Jeffrey, 1926–
    A truthful injustice
    1. Detective and mystery stories
    I. Title
    823.9'14 [F]

    ISBN 0-7278-5614-6

Typeset by Palimpsest Book Production Ltd.,
Polmont, Stirlingshire, Scotland.
Printed and bound in Great Britain by
MPG Books Ltd., Bodmin, Cornwall.

One

The phone rang and Wyatt picked up the cordless receiver, switched it on, raised the short aerial. 'Simon Wyatt speaking.' Charlotte said he identified himself as if delivering a benediction. Sisters delighted in trying to deflate brothers.

'It's Hilary, Mr Wyatt.'

He tried to put a person to the name.

'I'm not phoning from home because Vicky's there and I didn't want her to hear me. I said I had to go out to the supermarket and buy some things. I don't know whether I ought to be saying this . . .'

The mention of his daughter's name enabled him to place the caller. Hilary Pernell, one of Victoria's closer friends, who forever seemed to be in slight turmoil. 'Is something wrong?'

'She wouldn't like me telling you, but don't you agree . . .'

Hilary had the habit of frequently not finishing a sentence, leaving her listener to decide whether the unspoken words would have had any relevance.

'If you'd say what the problem is, I'd be better able to give an opinion.' He was annoyed with himself because he must have sounded pompous.

'She turned up in a terrible state and I thought . . .'

'What happened?' he demanded sharply.

1

'But I'm trying to tell you.'

'Sorry.'

'It's so difficult for me.'

It was proving far from easy for him. 'What has upset Vicky?'

'I thought at first there must be something terribly wrong with Leo—'

He interrupted what might have become a completed sentence. 'Is Leo ill?'

The birth of his grandson had brought him only pleasure, unlike the birth of his daughter.

'He's quite all right. When he was playing with my Henry, he became so boisterous we had to separate them and calm them down . . .'

He listened with sharp impatience to a disconnected description of events and finally interrupted her again. 'You said Vicky was in a terrible state when she arrived at your house. Why was she?'

'It's hardly surprising, is it?'

'I wish I knew. Why was she so upset?'

'I really shouldn't be telling you. I mean, she made me promise not to say anything.'

'Hilary, will you please tell me why Vicky was upset?'

'It's not that she or Leo is badly hurt, but to think he could . . . She first tried to tell me she'd fallen in the kitchen, but when I asked her how and where exactly, she began to cry.'

'How badly hurt is she?'

'It's more bruising than anything, I'm sure of that. But I still think she ought to have seen a doctor, just to be certain. But she simply wouldn't.'

'How was she hurt?'

'She . . .' After a brief pause, the words came in a rush; having nerved herself to betray a confidence, she hastened to complete that betrayal as quickly as possible. Frank, Victoria's husband, had come home late in the afternoon and had clearly been drinking heavily. He'd ignored both her and Leo, who had eagerly been waiting in the hall, having heard the car return, and had lurched through to the pantry where the drink was kept. He'd poured himself a large whisky, drunk that neat, poured another. Victoria – not a red-head for nothing – had said that if he didn't stop drinking, he'd make a complete fool of himself. He'd shouted that in his house he would do as he liked, to which she'd responded it was her house, not his. He'd called her a stuck-up bitch who considered herself so much better than he, she had replied that right then he was proving her correct. Swearing, he'd hit her several times and she'd fallen. Leo had begun to scream. He'd shouted at Leo to shut up and when, naturally, this had made him even more frightened, had hit him. She had picked up Leo and fled. After confessing what had happened, she'd made Hilary swear she would never ever tell another soul which was why she – Hilary – hadn't known what to do. On the one hand . . .

'It was your duty to break that promise,' Wyatt assured her.

'You really think so?'

'Of course.'

'That's what I decided,' she said, all doubts apparently dispelled by his certainty. 'It's a terrible state of affairs, isn't it?'

'Yes.'

'Don occasionally has a little too much to drink at the club, but that just makes him cheerful in rather a stupid way and . . . He's never once tried to hit me. One reads about this sort of thing, but never expects actually to meet it, does one?'

3

'No.'

'But then, of course, not everyone is like . . . Well, not been brought up . . . After Vicky calmed down, I told her I had to go out to the supermarket because I decided I must phone and tell you what had happened.' Doubts returned. 'I do hope you really think it was right . . .'

'Where is she now?'

'Here, as I said. She's staying the night . . . Before phoning you, I tried to work out the best thing to do from everybody's viewpoint. If Don had been at home . . . Except how could I have talked it over with him without being worried she might hear us . . . ?'

'You've done exactly the right thing.'

'I'm so relieved that's what you think. It's been so difficult . . . You will make certain she never even suspects I told you, won't you?'

'Yes,' he wearily answered.

'She'd never forgive me . . . It was the right thing to tell you?'

'Yes,' he answered, even more wearily.

'Then as soon as I ring off, I'll buy some broccoli because I haven't any vegetables in the house for the meal – and I did say I had to go out to buy something so I really should . . .'

He thanked her for phoning him, assured her yet again she could not be criticized for what she'd done, said goodbye and switched off the phone.

He drummed with his fingers on the kidney-shaped pedestal desk, which reputedly had come from Lord Beaconsfield's home. How best to deal with the situation – if possible, without betraying Hilary. Victoria would never admit what had happened, not only because she prided herself on always being able to cope unaided with life, but also because she could be certain he would be

4

thinking how right he'd been when he'd told her he thought it would be a mistake for her to marry Frank Tobin. 'Get with today,' had been her response. 'It's the twenty-first century, not the eighteenth. What the bloody hell do different backgrounds and environments matter now?' Sadly, she had learned one answer. But would she accept she had?

Was he making a disastrous mistake in deciding he should take positive action? There was seldom room for a referee in a marriage. But this might well not be an isolated incident, merely the latest and worst. That could explain why over the past months Victoria had shown little of the zest for life she had once possessed. Recently, he'd read that the rate of marriage breakdowns in the police force was higher than in almost any other section of the population. The cause was held to be the macho culture. Sentiment was a weakness, drinking with the boys was more important than going home to the wife and kids because it forged ever stronger bonds with those on whom one had to rely when working, women were sex symbols, and if a WPC refused a quick one around the corner, ten to one she was a lessie . . .

He'd always judged Tobin's cockiness to be a mark of resentment, his left-wing politics a way of squaring self-respect with the fact that he owed his unusually comfortable lifestyle more to his wife than to himself. Perhaps he often indulged in domestic violence because that was the only way in which he could get the better of Victoria; intellectually, he would always be the loser . . .

Wyatt found he'd clenched his fists. He unclenched them. He'd gain nothing, get nowhere, by sitting at the desk in the library and imagining the worst; he had to decide whether to try to help Victoria and if so, how . . .

Perhaps he should first accept his opinions were often too sharply edged; few people were as good or as bad as he could paint them. Victoria had fallen in love with Tobin and so she must once, at least, have found much in him that was admirable. Could he identify the other's better side and play on that in a way that would make him realize how appalled Victoria had been to be physically assaulted, along with Leo, in her own home? Could that be done without his believing the words to be a snide reference to his background?

Wyatt stood. Lacking any better idea, he decided he would drive over to Thornbry and talk to Tobin. He would show understanding; not even hint that Victoria had emotionally and financially brought so much to the marriage; and not react to any smart-alecky remark – the last, the hardest task. Tobin epitomized so much of what he disliked about the contemporary world, a world in which so many of the values he had been brought up to observe had been cast aside, in which a confessed drug addict and Lothario pop-star was viewed as an icon by hundreds of thousands . . . The scorn with which Victoria would greet such thoughts!

He left the panelled library and went into the hall, notable for the anachronistic staircase with its heavy, carved balusters that had been scornfully condemned by a visiting expert asked to survey the building in order to give an opinion on its architectural history. Personally, he viewed the staircase as an amusing Victorian addition, an extravagance rather than a pretentious attempt to suggest this was a mansion.

He climbed the stairs and went along the right-hand corridor to the end bedroom. Beamed ceiling, oak tester bed, beautifully inlaid mahogany dressing table, two Sheraton painted chairs, and large Sarouk rug provided a mixture broad enough further to annoy the architectural expert. Serena had laughingly dismissed the zealous regard for coherence – she loved the beauty and workmanship of the past and saw no harm in mixing periods.

She sat in the wide bed, propped up by pillows.

'How are you feeling?' he asked, as he came to a stop by the side of the bed, his head bent to clear the heavily carved canopy.

'Much better. In fact, I was just getting ready to come down.' She reached across and took hold of his hand. 'I'm sorry to have been even more of a useless wife.'

'We'd agreed, no more apologies.'

'You pronounced, I did not agree.' She briefly squeezed his hand. 'And anyway, just occasionally I dare to ignore my lord and master . . . Wouldn't it make Vicky furious to hear me say that!' She smiled.

'And how!' Was it coincidence she had mentioned Victoria, or had there been half-formed, hazy, and on his part unwanted, marital telepathy between them? 'You're sure you're fit enough to get up?'

'Quite certain. The doctor said it wasn't a particularly bad flu this year.'

'Doctors . . .' He stopped.

'Are sometimes right.'

But sometimes terribly wrong. 'I have to go out. I'll try not to be long. Would you prefer to stay in bed until I get back?'

'I'll be much better up and about. Where are you off to?'

'Charlotte needs some advice.'

'It's her finances again?'

'I gather so. Ironically, I don't think she ever acts on what I suggest. Perhaps she only asks me in order to discover what she won't do.'

7

'Vicky always says it's difficult to believe you and she are brother and sister.'

'Why so?'

'You'll have to ask her. I've always thought the two of you had quite a lot in common . . . Vicky hasn't been in touch today, has she?'

'No.'

'I wondered whether to ask the family to lunch on Sunday and I'd get a sirloin from the butcher's . . . Oh! Not a very good idea. She still won't let Leo eat beef. Strange how she's so frightened about the scare when normally she just laughs at such things.'

'If someone told her there was one chance in a million chocolate would give Leo blue spots between his eyes, she'd make certain he didn't have another piece.'

'Yet when she was younger, she went out of her way to take risks.'

'Yes.' He spoke more sharply than he'd intended.

'I wasn't thinking of Frank. I'm sure that's all turned out much better than you thought it possibly could. They're happy and couldn't love Leo more.'

'I hope so.'

'What an extraordinary thing to say! You've no reason to think they don't, have you?'

He hesitated.

'Well?'

'Of course not.'

'Then relax and stop thinking the worst of Frank.'

'To hear is to obey.'

'Like hell it is where you're concerned . . . Don't be away any longer than you have to be, sweet.'

'I'll be as quick as possible, but Charlotte does love to talk.'

'Of course she does when she's lonely. Why doesn't she

join the Women's Institute or something similar where she can meet people?'

'She's probably happier on her own, even if lonely. As she said once when I suggested something of the sort, could I see her submitting to being shown how to make prune wine by an elderly busybody with clacking teeth?'

'Only with the greatest difficulty. Your sister is hardly one of the easiest people to please . . . Go off now and then you'll be back before it's very late.'

'I'll hitch my steed to Eos's chariot.'

'Then be careful when you slip the reins or you'll end up in Norway.'

'I think you have me travelling in the wrong direction.'

She swung herself round and reached her feet out on to the ground, stood; she gripped both his hands. 'Have I told you how much you mean to me, Simon?'

'Many times, but not too often.'

'You've been so wonderful.'

'Even when I'm a crotchety bore?'

'You're never that for me. Mary was going on and on the other day about the problems Tom gives her and how all men are trouble. It was difficult not to tell her I must be married to an exception.'

'Just as well you desisted, or she'd have laughed uproariously. She calls me a boring ancient.'

'If she really does, it's only because you've never shown any desire to run your hands under her skirt.'

'Are you suggesting she'd welcome that?'

'It's never occurred to you that she likes men to make advances so she can enjoy the pleasure of slapping them down?'

'No, I can't say I have pondered that possibility. You're opening a whole new window on our friends.'

9

'You're rather unobservant.'

'So ancient, I'm no longer curious.'

She kissed him suddenly, then moved back. She spoke in a low voice. 'I feel so awful . . .'

'Don't.'

'You don't know what I was going to say.'

'So awful because we sleep in different rooms.'

'I . . . I've tried . . .'

'We're fit – when the flu's not around – Victoria still speaks to us even though we are her parents, Leo is a lovely little demon, and we can afford to live in a beautiful old house, all of which makes us unusually fortunate.'

'It's so difficult for you.'

'A sage wrote that true happiness is only to be found in overcoming difficulties.'

'That's stupid.'

'Sagacity is the forebear of stupidity.'

'You're talking nonsense because you're embarrassed by what I'm trying to say – that you are a husband in a million.'

'I'm only rated that highly?'

'You think you'd look good in a halo? . . . Go and see Charlotte and advise her to do the opposite of what you think she should.'

He left, reached the head of the stairs before he remembered the message he should have given her. He returned to the bedroom. She had stripped, preparatory to putting on clean underwear, and he suffered the brief, bitter memory of the first time he had seen her naked – his naive surprise that it was not only her head hair that was Titian red – and the passion which had followed. 'I forgot to mention,' he said, conscious of a sudden thickening of his voice, 'that Enid has made a shepherd's pie for our supper because she thought you'd be staying in bed.'

'Bless her!'

'Except when she drops a bottle of Latour eighty-four.'

'She was very upset.'

'Not nearly as much as I was.'

She chuckled as she stepped into a pair of lace-edged, lime-coloured pants.

'Am I allowed to share your amusement?'

'You were so furious, you scared her and so the next day the poor soul arrived with a bottle and wanted to give it to you to make up for the loss. I managed to persuade her to leave me to present it to you.'

'I don't remember receiving it.'

'It was Bulgarian plonk. I doubt you'd have understood it was the thought that counted, not the contents.' She slipped on her brassiere, reached up behind her back to secure the eyes. 'The next day, she asked me how you'd enjoyed it. I told her your silence was eloquent.'

'Devious.'

'Necessarily tactful. If she'd felt her generosity had been slighted, she might have refused to continue to work here. Good dailies are becoming ever more difficult to find.'

'A far more important consideration than her proclivity to splatter the floor with priceless nectar?'

'Of course. Are you still annoyed?'

'Anyone who has seen Latour coating the floor is entitled to be sulphuric for months afterwards.'

She half turned to face him. 'I didn't tell you immediately about the plonk because you were so annoyed; just like a dog which has its bone taken away.'

'The comparison does me credit.'

'I wasn't deceiving you. When we married, we promised each other we'd always tell the truth and I always have . . . Eventually.'

11

'As I have.' The lie came easily.

She crossed to the corner chair – which added yet one more period to the bedroom's furniture – on which lay the rest of her clothes. She slipped the silk petticoat over her head and wriggled to make it settle down her body. 'Once Vicky asked me – it was when she was in one of her more difficult phases – how we could be so happy in a world that was drowning in unhappiness. I told her we found happiness in our absolute trust for each other. Of course, she jeered at such a sloppy sentiment, but I think in her heart, she understood.'

'You always were an optimist.'

'One of us has to be . . . I always hope she and Frank have absolute trust in each other.'

Hope was the opium of the optimist. 'I'd better move.'

'You will change before you leave, won't you?'

'Why?'

'You can't go in that old shirt even if it is only your sister who'll see it. Why on earth are you wearing it?'

'I've been doing some gardening, much to John's disapproval, gardeners being so very territorial.'

'You look as if you've been submarining through the flower beds . . . If you need an excuse not to stay too late, tell Charlotte I'm being a clinging wife.'

'She wouldn't believe that.'

'She probably would, since she has a poor opinion of people.'

'Tim was responsible for much of that.'

'I never could understand why they split up.'

'Other people's romances are always inexplicable.'

'But not one's own?'

He smiled. 'They're just incomprehensible.'

He left. He was en route to Ronefield before he realized he had not changed his shirt.

Two

W yatt liked large and reasonably fast cars, but seldom drove the Volvo at speed. It might have been
concluded he flaunted his wealth, but he merely liked to
enjoy the comfort money could buy and was indifferent,
even hostile, to the modern cult of perceived equality.
Had he motored more, he would have bought a Bentley.

He slowed, turned left at the T-junction. Fifty yards
on, the lane curved sharply before it ran through woods
which had once been regularly pollarded, but now were
left to grow unchecked because there was so little profit
in cut logs. The woods gave way to hedge-bordered fields
and he braked to a halt in a natural lay-by. He picked up
the mobile from the front passenger seat, switched it on,
raised the aerial, dialled.

'Yes?' Charlotte said curtly, as always seeming to
expect the telephone call to present a challenge.

'Simon.'

'I'm glad you've phoned. I've had Molly badgering
me for information concerning Great-great-grandfather
Robert. I can't remember anything about him, but I
said you might since you seem to find our ancestors
interesting.'

'Which you don't.'

'When they led such God-awful, conventional, boring
lives?'

13

'One of them drank himself to death in Jamaica.'

'So what could be more boring than that?'

'Drinking oneself to death in Brixton . . . Who's Molly?'

'You're saying you can't remember?'

'I am.'

'She's a second cousin and you met her here last summer. You have a sieve of a memory.'

'Which acts as a kindly filter. But I do now seem to recall a tall, thin woman with prominent teeth, a corncrake's voice, and a total inability to understand when her listener was becoming very bored.'

'She's drawing up a genealogical chart of the family going back to King Canute.'

'Then I suppose I'd better see if there's any reference to Robert in the papers I've got. But only on condition I don't have to meet the lady again.'

'Coward.'

'An expert in self-preservation . . . Charlotte, will you do me a favour and play the guardian angel?'

'Again? Rather overdoing things at your age.'

'This is different.'

'It always is, according to the male.'

'If Serena rings . . .'

'As an accommodating sister, I'll feed her the agreed story that I've run out of cigarettes and, being the perfect gentleman we all know you to be, you've gone down to the pub to buy me a pack.'

'Ring my mobile if she does get in touch.'

'And you'll ring her and assure her you're safe and sound and just enjoying a quick pint in the local. Have you a recording of pub noise to play for the sake of veracity?'

'I shouldn't be very long.'

'Wham, bam, that's all, ma'am?'

'It's not like that.'

'The truth's painful?'

'I'll get back on to you to say when there's no need to cover for me any longer.'

'Don't do an Errol Flynn on us.'

Her crude forthrightness still had the capacity to surprise and annoy him. He switched off the mobile, switched on the car lights, started the engine and drove out of the lay-by on to the road.

Thornbry was a small town by the Channel. Originally confined to the foot of the hills which backed it, in the past ninety years houses had been built on the more moderate slopes and Victoria had chosen a house with a panoramic view of the sea – an expensive property if compared with the equivalent down on the level and without a view. He had bought the house as a wedding present; Victoria had been disagreeably surprised that he had not in addition promised her a generous monthly allowance. Her regard for the iniquities of inequality was limited.

He slowed to round the S-bend which led into the narrow one-way High Street, still lined with small shops. At the end of the road was a small roundabout and he took the road to the left which almost immediately climbed steeply; at the crossroads on the crest, he turned right. Athin Road, named after a forgotten and unlamented councillor, wriggled as it followed the contours, then straightened; number 12 was halfway along the straight section. The house lay below the level of the road and because the turning area in front of it was small, unless one had the use of the garage to increase the space of the swing, it was easier to leave the car parked on the road.

He crossed the pavement, opened the ornate wrought-iron gate, walked carefully down the flagstone path, using

15

the handrail for security. The coming meeting was one he would have given much to avoid, but for someone of his character, to wish not to do something was good reason for doing it.

The front door was painted a dark green, Victoria's favourite colour. When she wore a green dress rather than scruffy jeans, the contrast between that and her red hair added a touch of glamour to her attractive but strong features. He had never understood why she so seldom took the trouble to present herself in the best possible light and had once made the mistake of saying so. 'You've time-travelled from the dinosaur age,' had been her caustic, incoherent reply. He rang the bell and from inside came the sound of the chimes which had been installed before he'd bought the house. He would have had them removed, she left them because 'Nothing's more suburban, which is simply great.' He couldn't understand that either; or why she'd refused to have the antique furniture from her old bedroom; or why she'd married Frank Tobin when there had been so many other, better choices. Serena and he had sensed, without being able to explain on what grounds, that there was a dark side to his nature which he tried to hide under cockiness.

He rang the bell again. Lights were on in the hall, but that was no indication Tobin was at home. According to him, burglaries were up and clear-up rates down because as the wealthy grew wealthier, there was more to steal and therefore every security device had to be used to try to keep the thieves at bay.

He rang the bell a third time. Had he mentally geared himself up for an unpleasant meeting for nothing? He was about to turn away and walk back to the car when he heard muffled sounds from inside. Seconds later, Tobin shouted: 'Clear off, whoever you are.'

In her late teens, Victoria had brought home a wide variety of male types, ranging from hippies to the supercilious superior. Serena and he had liked some, disliked some, and fervently hoped she would not prolong her friendship with Tobin.

When it had become clear the friendship was not only continuing but strengthening, he had tactfully – he hoped – and forgoing any criticism, observed to her that someone whose behaviour was so often provocatively different from that which she met at home, might suggest a difficult future relationship. 'You don't even try to understand,' she'd said with bitter anger. 'He comes from a one-parent family and his mother never had any money. So of course he resents wealth.' Tobin's resentment didn't prevent his accepting each and every benefit the Wyatt connection provided . . . 'Frank, it's Simon.'

'Who?'

'Simon.'

'What d'you want?'

'To talk to you.'

'I've better bloody things to do.' He slurred his words.

'Please open the door.'

'Piss off.'

Wyatt gripped the handle, intending to rattle the door in the bizarre hope that this would persuade Tobin to do as asked; he found the door was unlocked. He stepped into the hall that was virtually unfurnished because Victoria had decided to follow the latest fad in interior decorating.

'I'll nick you for . . . for forced entry.' Tobin, face slackened from drink, was having trouble in keeping his balance, as well as speaking.

'When force was unnecessary?' Wyatt said, hoping a touch of levity would lighten the situation.

'You think you're so bleeding smart, don't you?'

'No, I don't make that mistake.'

'And I'm a dumb bastard.'

A soft answer turneth away wrath, but Wyatt's quick temper seldom allowed him to remember that. 'You're seldom dumb; your parentage is no concern of mine.'

Tobin swore at length.

'Hilary Pernell rang me earlier. She told me . . .'

'That she wanted screwing by a real man, not that poncy husband of hers.'

'She says you and Victoria had a very serious argument.'

'Given the chance, you'd screw her sore, wouldn't you?'

Wyatt struggled to subdue his anger and continue as planned, quietly, reasonably, persuasively. 'I know there are always going to be arguments in a marriage and . . .'

'I'll let you into a secret, Mr Wyatt, esquire, you know as much about life as a dead worm.'

'But however much one argues . . .'

'No woman tells me to stop drinking. Got it?'

'She was very concerned for you . . .'

'She don't give a sod for me.'

'You can't understand why she was so worried?'

'Yeah. She'd caught her tits in the mangle.'

'She was very worried because, I expect, experience had taught her that when you become drunk, you get violent.'

'Who's talking about being violent?'

'You assaulted her violently.'

'Wasn't no more than a Saturday night tickle to persuade her to belt up. Like I told her, when I want a drink, I'll bleeding well have one and no slag is

18

going to tell me different. And I want one right now.'
He turned.

'You'll listen to what I have to say . . .'

He farted. 'And that's what I've got to say, squire.'
He moved too quickly and had to reach to the wall for
support. He made his stumbling way down the corridor
into the kitchen and the pantry beyond where it took him
time and much cursing to open a bottle of whisky and
three-parts fill a glass. He spoke with stumbling words.
'I'd offer you one, squire, seeing it might help you climb
down off your high horse, only the likes of you don't drink
anything but champagne. I've got champagne, of course I
have, but I'm not wasting it on you.' He raised the glass,
took time to find his mouth.

'You admit you struck Victoria earlier?'

'Had to teach her some manners, didn't I?'

'And you also struck Leo?'

'Had to stop the little bastard screaming.'

'Do you attack anyone when you're drunk or only
women and children who can't hit back?'

'I'll hit an old man if you don't get out of my house,
bloody fast.'

'This is my daughter's house.'

'What's hers is mine; just understand that, squire. So
shove off.'

'I warn you that if you hit or threaten either Victoria
or Leo again, I will report you to the police.'

'I am the police, Detective Sergeant Me. Don't like to
remember that, do you? You think a policeman's a social
dustman, sweeping up the human rubbish so it doesn't
dirty your shoes. Never been good enough for the likes
of your daughter, have I?'

'If a man strikes a woman and a child, he's not good
enough for anyone's daughter, dustman or duke.'

19

'You a holy, preaching what a bloody wonderful world this would be if only everyone would love everyone else? Kick a holy in the goolies and see how much he loves you. Hypo . . . hypocrites, that's what the whole sodding lot of you civilians are.' He waved his hands to add emphasis to his words and forgetting he held the glass. Whisky splashed on to the wall. 'Look what you've done!' he shouted.

'By telekinesis?'

'I've had enough of smart-arse. I'm going to throw you out of my house. My house.'

Wyatt was unprepared for Tobin's rush with arms outstretched and received a glancing blow to his cheek before Tobin crashed into him with a force that would have sent him flying had he not been so close to the table in the centre of the kitchen. His shirt collar was grabbed and twisted and he had difficulty in breathing until the collar tore free, causing Tobin to stagger backwards. 'For God's sake . . .' he began, as Tobin hurled himself forward, arms flailing.

Instinct made Wyatt fight back and for a few seconds he was hitting out, then Tobin tripped over his own legs and collapsed to the ground.

Wyatt, short of breath, trembling slightly from emotional shock and alarm, gripped the table for support as he suffered a sense of coruscating humiliation at the knowledge he had fought with his son-in-law.

Tobin lay on the floor, staring up. 'Are you all right?' Wyatt finally asked, concerned by the other's immobility. 'D'you need a hand to get up?'

'I need a drink.'

'That's the last thing you require.'

'You kicked me down.'

'You fell over your own legs.'

'You bleeding kicked me. Can't even fight straight, your kind can't.'

'Can you understand what I'm saying?'

'I'm going to chuck you out of my house.'

'It will be best for all concerned if we forget what's just happened.'

Tobin finally moved and struggled to regain his feet; despite the lack of coordination between brain and muscle, he eventually stood. He aimed a wild swing at Wyatt, missed by inches, lost all balance because of the wasted momentum and once more collapsed on to the floor.

Wyatt left.

Three

Ronefield – it was said rone was once the dialect name for the ragstone that had been locally quarried – consisted of a handful of old houses, twenty council houses and bungalows, a dozen privately owned modern houses, a general store and sub post-office forever on the point of closing because of loss of trade to the nearby towns' supermarkets, a bakery converted into a house, a garage now an office, a butcher with a surprisingly large trade – the meat was actually what it claimed to be – and a public house that was becoming less and less profitable as the penalties for drink-driving became more draconian. No longer the tiny, relatively remote village it had once been, now inhabited by people who commuted rather than worked on the land, it had lost its previous identity and failed to gain a new one.

Bray's Cottage was a small seventeenth-century farm-house, half a mile to the east of Ronefield, on ground sufficiently elevated to provide a partial view of the surrounding countryside. The headlights of the Volvo picked out the entrance to the short drive and Wyatt turned into this, braked to a stop in front of the garage doors. He left the car, not bothering to take a torch because the moon was sufficiently full to enable him easily to walk round to the garden gate and then the front door. He used the knocker and immediately a dog started barking.

A curtain was withdrawn to spill light over him, bolts were withdrawn and the door was opened; Isser, a Lakeland terrier, barked a couple more times, decided it knew him, pawed his leg, asking to be stroked.

Charlotte studied him. 'You look as if you've been reading and re-reading the *Kama Sutra* from cover to cover.'

He stepped into the hall, closed the door.

'Your collar's gone and your cheek looks rough. Did the husband come home too soon?'

'A drunken sot attacked me. I need a drink.' After he'd spoken, he realized he'd repeated Tobin's words.

He went into the sitting room as she turned right to go into the kitchen. He sat in one of the comfortable armchairs and stared at the inglenook fireplace in which a small fire burned, more for the cheerfulness than the heat. Time and memory were a mystery. It was only half an hour since he'd left Athin Road, but already it seemed long ago because images were blurred and as if recalled from a nightmare rather than reality.

She entered the room, Isser trotting by her side. She handed him one glass, crossed to a second chair, sat. 'Are you in trouble?' she asked quietly.

'Not in the way you think,' he answered, knowing that if he really had been threatened by a drunken husband, she would have disagreed with his actions, yet stood by him. She had a direct manner, often a sharp tongue, and a readiness to face facts rather than try to sidestep them; she possessed a sense of family loyalty strong enough to overcome her own judgement of what was morally right and wrong.

'Are you going to tell me?' she finally asked.

'Earlier in the evening, Hilary Pernell phoned me – she's a great friend of Vicky's.' He drank.

'I've met her. Scatty but pleasant, married to a prune.'

'She told me Vicky and Frank had had a row because of his drinking; it became heated and he hit her, then when Leo started crying, hit him to shut him up.'

She stared at him, her expression taut. 'The bastard!'

'She left home with Leo and went to Hilary's place; said why she was there and made Hilary promise not to tell me. But Hilary rang to say what had happened. I told Serena I was coming to see you because you needed some advice, drove over to Thornbry to talk to Frank . . .'

'Then it was you who needed advice, not me.'

'How d'you mean?'

'With your quick temper, the worst thing you could have done was go straight over and curse him.'

'I ought to have let him get away with it?'

'To have taken the time to calm down and work out how best to deal with a difficult situation rather than rush off to a confrontation that was almost bound to end in physical violence.'

'Who said it did?'

'You left home in a shirt lacking its collar? You bruised your own cheek? You needed a drink so badly because you were thirsty? Come off it.'

'He was drunk up to his eyeballs.'

'That surprised you?'

'I gathered he drank, but not like that . . . Despite what you think, I very calmly pointed out that hitting a woman and a child was not the way to behave . . .'

'Which must have increased his alcoholic blood pressure to straining point. For God's sake, Simon, you know how he's always reacted to the slightest hint that he's not cut out to be married to Vicky.'

'He told me he'd only given Vicky a Saturday night tickle. He seemed to think that justified hitting her.'

'Perhaps for him it did.'

'He hit Leo to stop him crying. He tried to order me out of his house . . . "His" house.'

'Legally, these days it probably will be half his. Women didn't think of that side of things when they started chucking their bras around.'

'He was blind drunk . . .'

'So you said.'

'And tried to throw me out. There was a bit of a fracas.'

'You were mad to try to take on someone half your age and twice your strength.'

'I didn't take him on.'

'So?'

'He fell over his own feet. I offered to help him up . . .'

'Ever the perfect gentleman!'

'He managed to get to his feet and immediately took a swing at me, missed, collapsed to the floor again. So I left.'

'Common sense finally filtered through!'

'I couldn't return home immediately or Serena would have wanted to know why my shirt was torn and why I was so on edge. I'd have had to tell her what had happened and that would have upset her most terribly. She's convinced herself that Vicky's marriage is still all gold.'

'Some self-deception!'

'You know how emotional she is.'

'She can be a whole lot stronger than you seem to think when the need arises. I'll explain why. Unlike men, women don't regard pleasure as their right.'

'You don't understand . . .'

'You're old enough to remember the days when marriage was for better or worse and not for a couple of months. You must have known good times, but can't or won't face the bad ones.'

'I've never before realized how much you disapprove.'

'You think I should approve of your regularly betraying your marriage?'

'If you're so critical, why do you cover for me?'

'I'm your sister.'

'Blood is thicker than muddied water?'

She did not answer.

They were silent for a while. He finished his drink, then said: 'I'd better move or Serena will start imagining a car crash and start panicking. I can't return home looking like this or she'll want to know how the collar was torn off. You often wear men's shirts, so can you let me have one?'

'It'll be far too large around the chest – Mother always said I was a big girl – but I suppose it'll be better than nothing . . . But I suggest you don't return until you've calmed right down and can appear to be reasonably composed and relaxed. Another drink would help.'

'I shouldn't, not since I have to drive home.'

'Surely, it's become a habit to do what you shouldn't?'

She had always been too direct, even when young, just as she had seldom bothered about her appearance – she was wearing a faded shirt, jeans, and had used no make-up. Serena said Vicky had sideways inherited this lack of dress pride.

She crossed to where he sat and held out her hand for his glass. 'A penny for them.'

'Too valuable to be sold.'

She took the glass, but did not move. 'You sounded just like Father then. Do you remember that was always his answer if anyone asked him what he was thinking?'

'Was it?'

'And how it annoyed Mother! . . . However much they argued, however annoyed they became with each other, as kids we never had to wonder if there was any real trouble between them, did we?'

'Of course not.'

'Shows how lucky we were.' She turned and left the room.

It was true that they had never doubted their parents' happiness, he thought. But was that because it was fact or had the truth been hidden from them? Perhaps they were lucky not to know the answer.

The door of Serena's bedroom was ajar. 'Are you awake?' he said quietly enough that were she asleep, she would not be awakened.

'Come in.'

The bedside light was switched on as he entered. 'How are you feeling?'

'Virtually back to normal and I'll be up and about tomorrow. How's Charlotte?'

'Same as ever.'

She patted the bed and he sat. She favoured lacy, diaphanous nightdresses and her neat breasts were hazily visible, making them more intriguing than if they had been bare. He wondered if she could understand how he longed to fondle them preparatory to full sex and not the substitute for it which they sometimes pursued and which left him unsatisfied and, he could be certain, her bitterly self-critical.

'Did you remember to give her the opposite advice to that which you thought she ought to take?'

'In a roundabout way.'

'Of course, she can be so unpredictable that one day she may do exactly as you suggest and then you'll be blamed when things go wrong . . . She gave you supper, of course?'

'No.'

'You haven't eaten? Why on earth didn't you ask her for something?'

'I didn't think about it.'

'It's not like you to ignore meal times . . . You're not starting my flu, are you?'

'Not as far as I can judge.'

'But you do seem a bit . . . Well, on edge.'

He should have risked a third drink. 'Just tired. I stayed chatting longer than I intended. Sorry if you began to worry.'

'I didn't really. I know what it's like when you two are together . . . I didn't eat half the shepherd's pie Enid made and it's very tasty, so you can heat that up in the microwave – don't forget to put cling over the dish and make a couple of holes to let out the steam. And there's one of those individual apple pies you like in the deep freeze which you can defrost and warm while you're having the first course. I think there's some cream left from lunch, but if there isn't . . .'

'It'll be much better for me.' He stood.

'What shirt are you wearing?' she asked.

Why did women so often notice things they weren't meant to? 'You told me to change so I got it out of the cupboard.'

'It doesn't look like one of yours.'

'Maybe I just haven't worn it for a long time.'

'Just as well, as it doesn't fit you and the pattern and colour certainly don't suit you . . . Enid can wash and iron it and I'll give it to the Salvation Army shop in Setonhurst. I'm not having you walk around dressed as badly as your sister.'

28

'I bow to authority.'

'Like hell you do!' She stared up at him and said slowly and with deep emotion: 'I wonder why I'm lucky enough to be married to someone so wonderfully loyal despite everything?'

She had the capacity, unknown to her, to pluck his conscience very hard.

Four

Mrs Aldrich was forty-three, a widow for seven years, and had to work hard to make ends meet, yet was of a cheerful disposition and did not resent the poor hand life had dealt her. On Wednesday and Friday mornings, she worked for the Tobins and started early, which suited everyone because she was on hand to help with Leo. She liked Mrs Tobin, a thoughtful and friendly employer, but Mr Tobin lacked both characteristics; he would give an order rather than make a request and whilst she accepted that this might be due to his job, she thought it more likely it was because he did not have his wife's social experience. Truth to tell, she disliked him and was glad his job meant he was seldom at home when she worked there

She didn't ride her bicycle up the hill (she was not that fit), but mounted it as soon as she reached the crest and Athin Road. As she approached No. 12, she looked forward to the cup of tea and the chocolate biscuit she would be offered on arrival to warm her up. There was a cold wind coming off the sea and although the drizzle had ceased, it looked as if it would soon start again.

She freewheeled down to the house, leaned her bike against the garage wall, walked along to the front door and rang the bell. When there was no response, she rang again. She briefly wondered if she'd forgotten the family was due to be away, decided she had not. Were they still all in bed? That seemed very unlikely with Leo as lively as a rave party. She went round to the side door, but it was locked. She experienced a vague feeling of disquiet and looked through the window; saw half of the empty kitchen. Mrs Tobin had wanted her to have a key to the side door so she could enter the house if and when the family was away, but Mr Tobin had vetoed the idea. She had been insulted by his evident belief that if she had the run of the house on her own, she would pinch something . . .

It seemed there could be no one at home even though she had not been warned this would be so. She made her way back to the garage and lifted her bike upright and then, because the disquiet had not gone away, did not wheel it up to the road, but along to the hall window. She looked through this and to her horror saw a body lying on the floor.

Metcalfe drove his four-year-old Fiesta into the car park at the side of the eight-storey divisional HQ, nominated the ugliest building in Setonhurst despite the stern competition. He parked against the small flower bed, not yet planted up, and thought that soon he would no longer mournfully have to turn out on a grey, overcast, drizzly day, but could stay at home and be mournful there.

He climbed out of the car, locked the doors, made his way across to the side entrance of the building. With retirement only weeks ahead, he ironically became less and less certain the future was to be welcomed. Had Gwen been alive, they would have enjoyed many of the pleasures they'd promised themselves – she longed to explore Scotland by car, he'd wanted to be in Paris in the spring because he'd always believed that the city

31

truly was touched with magic even though he'd been told by friends that Parisian waiters would strip all the magic even out of wonderland.

The lift was up at the eighth floor and he began his climb up stairs which wound around the lift shaft – in pursuit of economy, only one lift had been installed instead of the two needed; politicians demanded financial economy from all but themselves.

As he passed the detective inspector's door on the fifth floor, there was a shout. He retraced a couple of steps and went into a room overcrowded with filing cabinets, bookcase, desk, chairs, and general clutter. 'Morning, sir.' He came to a halt in front of the desk on which was an untidy heap of files of different sizes and colours.

'Tobin's been found dead,' Horner said abruptly.

'Good God! . . . What happened – an accident?'

'The PC who phoned reports Tobin's body was found in the hall. He'd suffered an injury to the head which does not appear to be extensive. There are bloodstains on the kitchen table . . .'

'Kitchen table?'

'The PC suggests that perhaps Tobin suffered a fall in the kitchen and this led to a heart attack when he was in the hall. We obviously won't know any more until we have the medical report. The constable got on to me, not uniform, because Tobin is one of us.'

'Frank's full young to suffer a heart attack,' Metcalfe observed.

'Quite. I said we'll handle this from now on. Do you know his home address?'

'He lives in Thornbry, but I can't say more than that.'

Horner picked up a sheet of paper and read. 'Athin Road. I haven't the number.' He dropped the paper, leaned back in the chair. He was well overweight – his wife was a good cook and he lacked the resolve to refuse second helpings. 'First thing is to find the wife and inform her.'

'She's not at home?'

'I've just said not,' Horner replied sharply.

The DI had not said so, but Metcalfe did not argue. Horner's character belied his appearance – he was not essentially a good-natured man with a sense of humour. 'He has a son – any sign of him?'

'None reported.'

'Maybe his missus and the kid left early in the morning.'

'No beds were unmade and for what it's worth, the constable reckoned he'd been dead for several hours. Do you know the wife?'

'I've met her a few times.'

'You wouldn't call yourself a personal friend of the Tobins?'

'No.'

'That helps when it comes to telling her.'

Horner was right, Metcalfe thought, but only to a small extent. Of all the tasks a policeman was called upon to do, the giving of bad news was perhaps the worst; too many times he had watched someone mentally crumple because of what he had just said; just as he had crumpled when told Gwen had not recovered consciousness after the operation.

'How old is the son?' Horner asked.

'Three, four, something like that.'

'Are things going to be rough for the wife?'

'Financially, probably not. She's from a wealthy family so one would hope they'd pitch in, if needed.'

'What family's that?'

He was surprised the detective inspector did not know, then was surprised that he should have been surprised.

Horner might once have been sharp enough to take an interest in the lives of his team – that was how a good one was welded together – but for quite some time he had suffered from wind-down; accepting he would gain no further promotion before retirement, his concern had become himself, not his work. 'They're the Wyatts who live at Bredgley Hall.'

'You sound as if I'm I supposed to be impressed?'

Only if he was interested in the history of the country-side and its buildings. 'The house is one of the oldest in the county, in part dating from the middle of the fourteenth century, reputedly built for a nephew of Mortimer, the lover of Isabella.'

'Who was she?'

'Mother of Edward the Third and she and Mortimer virtually ruled for three years until her son . . .'

'Never mind,' Horner said, in tones of someone who'd gratefully left history at school. 'Check with the uniform at Athin Road and if he hasn't located the wife, talk to the parents. I imagine you can speak Anglo-Saxon?'

Metcalfe wasn't certain whether that was meant to be humorous or sarcastic.

'I don't want her to find out from someone other than us or the parents – is that clear?'

'Yes, sir.'

Metcalfe left and went along the corridor past the detective sergeant's room, now without a tenant, to the CID general room, in which the perpetual degree of disorder – files stacked on the floor, recovered property not yet taken down to the Property Room and logged, photographs and memoranda not yet pinned up on the notice board – defied the ruling that it was to be neat and tidy at all times.

Seal was working a computer. Metcalfe said: 'Have you heard that Frank's died?'

'Christ! What the hell happened?'

He sat at his desk. 'The only information so far is he may have had a heart attack after suffering a head injury. They're waiting for the police surgeon.'

'You just never know. Yesterday he was full of himself, today he's full of nothing.'

Those words, Metcalfe thought, unwittingly revealed – Seal seldom thought before he spoke – the dislike many had had for the detective sergeant. Tobin had been by nature a bully, using rank to mark his superiority, but this had not been the main reason for the dislike; that was caused by the way in which he had repeatedly detailed the bonuses of being married to a woman from a wealthy family. His words had induced envy and contempt, the latter because the manner of his boasting had suggested he had married for money. 'Do you know the number of Frank's home?'

'No.'

He stood, threaded a way between the desks to the noticeboard on which in disorganized fashion were pinned memoranda, circulars, group photographs with one head circled in marking ink and a request for identification, details of coming social events, cartoons with a bearing on police work cut out from newspapers, duty rotas, and the addresses and phone numbers of CID members. He checked the details against Tobin's name, returned to his desk, dialled.

PC Bradley identified himself, then asked Metcalfe to give his own name and rank before he was willing to answer questions.

'Have you any lead on where the wife and kid are right now?' Metcalfe asked.

'None at all.'

'What about the neighbours – can they help?'

35

'I've not had the chance to talk to 'em. Orders were to stay in the house until after the preliminary medical examination and removal of the body. The surgeon's only just left.'

'So what's his verdict?'

'Refuses to give one.'

'Why's that?'

'He's worried because the injury to the head doesn't look much, on top of which Tobin was found in the hall. Says it'll need the PM to sort out the exact cause of death.'

'What about time?'

'Last night, between eight and eleven and like always, that can't be taken as accurate. I don't know why they bother to give a time when in the next breath they say it's only maybe.'

'But it's reasonably certain he died yesterday evening rather than this morning?'

'As I understand things.'

'So it's likely the wife and kid weren't at home last night, especially as none of the beds looked as if they'd been slept in?'

'I'll tell you what, mate, I'm not trying to do your job, but I reckon it'll be worth one of your lot having a look around.'

'Why so?'

'After I spoke to your guv'nor and said I couldn't answer any of his questions – got shafted for being incompetent – I had a look around the place. On the kitchen floor, mostly hidden, there's a piece of coloured material that's a collar torn off a shirt or I'm an organ grinder's monkey.'

'What have you done with it?'

'Left it where it is, of course.'

'Anything else that's interesting?'

'Only a smashed glass, a dampish stain on a wall, and what could be blood on the edge of the kitchen table – which would say how he got the injury to the head.'

'You saw him before he was carted off?'

'It was me what got called in.'

'Was his shirt lacking its collar?'

'No.'

'OK. I'll get back when there's something to tell.'

'Have I got to hang on here?'

'Until someone says different. If the wife turns up, we don't want her to hear the news from a neighbour.'

Metcalfe said goodbye, replaced the receiver, stared at the far wall with unfocused eyes.

'This bloody machine won't do what I want it to,' Seal said angrily, staring at the VDU on his desk.

'Must be a female model.'

A few minutes later, Metcalfe went along to the DI's room.

'Yes?' said Horner, as he looked up from a file.

'I've just had a word with PC Bradley who's at Tobin's house. The doc gave the usual warning about time of death, names between eight and eleven last night. No bed was unmade. So it looks like the wife and kid couldn't have been home yesterday evening onwards. The PC had a quick look around the place and says that on the kitchen floor is a torn piece of material which he identifies as a shirt collar.'

'From Tobin's shirt?'

'That was undamaged.'

Horner began to tap on the desk with his fingers. 'Is the PC staying there?'

'I said to do that until told different. In view of the

collar, I thought you might reckon it best if we check things out before there's any more movement.'

'How convinced is he that it's a shirt collar?'

'Can't be certain without picking it up and examining it closely, but doesn't reckon there's much room for doubt.'

'There's always room for doubt,' Horner snapped. He was annoyed. If Tobin's death could not be dealt with by filling in relatively few forms, he was faced with an investigation that might take time and effort. 'I'll send someone to the house. You talk to her parents and find out where she is and tell her the news.'

The massive wrought-iron gates, set in curved brick-work, were artistically elaborate; the long drive was lined with oaks which bore their centuries proudly; the house – two octagonal stacks with spiral brickwork, steep peg-tile roofs, small gables, beamed exterior top floor which overhung by a foot the lower one, massive, studded front door with heavily carved stone surround – came into ever sharper view. Metcalfe rounded the raised flower bed in the centre of the large turning circle and braked to a halt. Visible beyond the house to the left was a tithe barn which surely had been capable of storing the Church's claim on the produce of many hundreds of acres. Had Horner been with him, would he have experienced even a frisson of wonder at so clearly meeting the past, could he have imagined the pride that must accompany the ownership of such a property? Probably not. Horner lacked a romantic imagination.

He left the car and crossed to the front door which, close to, seemed strong enough to resist a battering ram. There was a wrought-iron knocker in the shape of a horse's head and on the side wall, a bell push. Ever the traditionalist, he knocked firmly.

The door was opened to the accompaniment of a tooth-twitching screech from the hinges and he faced a woman whose features even a Frenchman would have found difficulty in praising. 'Is Mr Wyatt in?'

'Who wants to know?' Her voice was touched with the local burr.

Of undiluted country stock, he decided; stock that through the centuries had accepted service without ever offering servility. 'Detective Constable Metcalfe, county CID.'

She had dark brown eyes – her one physical asset – and these recorded initial surprise and then careful assessment. 'You'd best come in.'

The hall disappointed him. He had expected space, a high, heavily beamed ceiling, a suit or two of armour, and patterns of weapons on the walls, but the area was small, the ceiling low and lightly beamed, and not a suit of armour or weapon in sight.

She showed him into a room large enough, with its huge open fireplace and carved marble mantel, to begin to meet his wishful image; the period furniture looked to be of the highest quality; the view through the three leaded windows was, even in March, one of natural beauty.

Five minutes later, a tall man, his face long and lean, his nose a shade too full, his generous mouth expressing in repose quiet humour, a plaster on his right cheek, dressed in old clothes which Metcalfe felt hardly suited the owner of such an architectural treasure, entered.

'Sorry to keep you waiting, but I was in the garden, working with John, and Enid couldn't find me.'

From which he gathered Wyatt was sufficiently keen a gardener to be prepared to get his hands dirty.

'Before you tell me what brings you here, can I offer you something?'

'Thank you, no, sir.' Many of the policemen younger than he never willingly addressed a civilian as 'sir'; he did so merely as a mark of good manners.

'Then have a seat.'

He sat very carefully on one of the four luxuriously covered fauteuils, not that he knew this was the name used by experts who understood the financial value of snobbism. He sensed in Wyatt a hint of uneasy worry, but saw no significance in that since a civilian often wondered, when a policeman called at his home, what past peccadillo was catching up with him.

'Is something wrong?' Wyatt asked.

'I'm afraid I have some very bad news.' There were two ways of imparting bad news – directly, so imagination had no time to blossom, or obliquely, so that the recipient might guess the truth and subconsciously prepare himself. He preferred the first. 'I'm afraid that earlier this morning, Detective Sergeant Tobin was found dead at his home.'

Expression strained, Wyatt stared at Metcalfe, then finally said wildly: 'That's impossible.'

'I'm afraid not.' A policeman soon learned that life and death walked hand in hand; civilians didn't and their ignorance left them very vulnerable. 'It's impossible to be positive before the PM, but it seems the likely cause of death was a heart attack, before or after a fall which occasioned injury to the head.'

'Then you . . .'

'I what, Mr Wyatt?'

Wyatt stood and crossed to the nearest window, stared out. After a moment, speaking more calmly, he said: 'Damned if I know what I was going to say. To tell the

40

truth, this has been such a hell of a shock, my mind's in chaos.'

'That's hardly surprising.'

'Thank you for coming here and telling me. Now, if you don't mind . . .'

'I'm sorry, but I need to know one or two things. Can you tell me where your daughter is?'

'Why do you ask?'

'She has to be told the tragic news.'

'My wife and I will see that she is.'

'That will be far better.' Metcalfe hoped that his relief was not obvious. 'I will in due course have to ask her a few questions.'

'Hardly the time for that.'

'I have to agree, Mr Wyatt, but I'm afraid there is a routine which has to be carried out.'

Wyatt turned and faced Metcalfe. 'Why?'

'Sudden deaths, when there is doubt about the cause, have to be investigated; apart from any other reason so that, where applicable, a general safety recommendation can be made to the public – naturally, without any reference to the identity of the victim.'

'My daughter wasn't at her home last night and so will be unable to tell you anything.'

'May I ask how you know she was not there?'

'She's been in touch to say she's staying with a friend.'

'Can you give me the friend's address?'

'I don't want my daughter to hear about Frank's death from you.'

'I assure you I will not speak to her until quite certain you or your wife has informed her.'

Wyatt hesitated, then said, 'Her name is Hilary Pernell. I don't know the address off-hand.'

'Would you be able to find it for me?'

Wyatt, his expression set, left the room. Very pleasant until his wishes were challenged, Metcalfe thought. A common trait amongst the rich.

Wyatt returned. 'The house is called Hopstand and it's just beyond the village of Festhurst.'

'Thank you, sir.'

When Metcalfe stepped out on to the drive, the cold wind had risen, the clouds had thickened, and the air held the dampness of more rain. Spring seemed a long way away. For the Wyatts' daughter, winter was just beginning.

Five

S erena drove the blue Astra into the right-hand garage, once part of the stables. She picked up her handbag and plastic carrier bag from the passenger seat, left the car, crossed the paved yard, and entered the house through the nearer back door. In the kitchen – equipped with every labour-saving device and the traditional Aga – she put the bag down on one of the working surfaces and brought out of it two polystyrene bottle containers, which she stood upright.

She crossed to the inner door, went through to the hall, and called out: 'Simon.'

The door of the drawing room opened and he hurried out. 'Thank God you've come back!'

'Did you imagine I'd decided to leave home?' she asked teasingly.

'Earlier on . . .'

'I've something for you.'

'I didn't know whether to go right away or wait for you.'

'Come on through to the kitchen and see your present . . .'

'Will you bloody listen.'

She was shocked by his harsh words.

He cursed himself for being so scared he had forgotten the need to break the news as gently as possible. 'I'm afraid . . .'

43

'What's wrong? What's happened?'

He took hold of her arm and eased her across to the doorway and into the drawing room.

'You've got to tell me,' she said, her voice high.

'Let's sit.'

He needed support as much as she would. That scuffle could not have caused Frank's death . . . Or could it? 'A detective came here earlier to give me some very bad news. He . . .'

'It's Vicky. She's in hospital . . .'

'No.'

'Leo's dying?'

'No.' Her escalating fears forced him to be far blunter than he wished. 'He told me Frank had been found dead in their house.' Watching her, he could judge how she was comforted momentarily because her worst fears had not been met, then suffered an emotional conscience that she could have found relief in the circumstances.

Her eyes filled with tears. 'Life can be so terribly cruel.'

Was a small part of herself included in that cry?

'He's too young . . . How could he have died?'

'He suffered some sort of fall in the house. We have to think what to do, as Vicky doesn't yet know.'

'She must do.'

'She wasn't at home.'

'Why not?'

'She spent the night at Hilary's.'

'How d'you know?'

He ignored the question. 'Before you got back, I was trying to decide whether to ring her . . .'

'You'd tell her over the telephone?'

'She must hear it from us, not the police. They say they have to question her. They've promised to make certain

44

we speak to her first, but they could forget. If we don't tell her quickly, they might.'

'They can't worry her at such a terrible time.'

'The law doesn't consider feelings.'

'You've got to tell them they can't do it.'

'They wouldn't listen. We have to tell Vicky now. One of us must phone . . .'

She spoke so violently, she was almost screaming. 'No phone. I'll drive there and explain. It's a mother's duty.'

'Then we'll . . .'

'I'm going on my own.'

'But you're naturally so upset . . .'

'On my own.'

He argued no further, certain that to do so would merely exacerbate her emotional stress.

She stood, hurried past him and out of the room. A moment later, he heard the Astra drive out of the yard.

He slowly made his way through to the kitchen and went into the pantry, poured himself a strong gin and tonic; he returned to the drawing room, sat. Vicky's marriage to Tobin had caused them considerable distress; Tobin's death threatened to cause very much more . . . Vicky had always had a wild side to her character. Serena had endlessly worried because of this, he had been far less troubled because he had believed Vicky possessed the saving grace of sufficient common sense to ring-fence that wildness. She had run away from boarding school, but left a note which made certain she was soon found; at the age of fourteen, she had announced she would start taking the Pill – none of Serena's surreptitious searches had ever found the slightest evidence of sexual activity; in her late teens, she had become politically conscious and joined demonstrations against the sins of capitalism – while continuing to live at home and enjoy them . . .

Yet when engaged to Roger Grover, who could have won a contest for the ideal son-in-law with both Serena and him, she had met Tobin when he had been policing one of the more ludicrous demonstrations and had soon afterwards married him, rejecting all their advice with the claim he offered life, not upper middle-class atrophy. If only that ring-fence had been as firm as he had once believed it to be . . . If only. The most useless expression in the language, he had used it again and again since Victoria had been born. If only her birth had not been so complicated, if only the doctor at the nursing home had not been so impatient and had enjoyed the professional humility to realize the need of someone with greater gynaecological skill than he possessed, if only Serena had not been left unable to enjoy normal sex . . . Not one second of the past could be altered. 'The Moving Finger writes; and, having writ, Moves on . . .'

He drained the glass, went back to the pantry and poured himself a second and stronger drink. Why had he failed to tell the detective he had been at the house the previous evening and he and Tobin had had a scuffle? he asked himself as he once more settled in the drawing room. An attempt to shield Serena from the truth? Fear that he might be held responsible for the death? But he had not started the scuffle, had done no more than defend himself, and at the conclusion the drunken Tobin had been physically unharmed . . .

He could not see the cordless receiver so went through to the hall and the telephone on the eighteenth-century lowboy, dialled.

'Yes?' said Charlotte, her initial manner as abrupt as ever.

'I need your help.'

'Serena won't think visiting me two days running is rather overdoing sibling affection?'

Her sarcasm suggested she'd backed a losing horse, a habit of hers. 'I've just had a detective here. He told me Frank died last night.'

'Good God! . . . Have you raised the flag?'

'That's sick.'

'Becoming pious in your old age?'

'He suffered an injury to his head, but they can't say for certain that was the cause of death before they hold a post-mortem.'

'If it was an accident, why d'you need my help?'

'Are you forgetting we had a scuffle?'

'Are you telling me you killed him?'

'Of course I'm bloody well not.'

'Swearing at a lady! You must be in a state.'

'What d'you expect?'

'The usual suave, friendly, slightly superior male disengagement.'

'Can't you take it seriously?'

'Frank's death? No.'

'But what will the police think if they learn about the scuffle?'

There was a silence which she finally broke. 'Simon, surely you told the detective what happened?'

'No.'

'Didn't you realize how dangerous that silence could be? Why didn't you tell the man? Too ashamed to admit you'd had a rough and tumble with a drunken son-in-law?'

'Because I was shocked by the news and afraid of how Serena would take it; because I wondered if I could possibly have been inadvertently responsible.'

'You've just said you couldn't have been.'

'I can think logically now; I couldn't then.'

'If the police discover you were in the house . . .'

'How can they possibly do so? Frank was on his own, no one called, the phone didn't ring, and you're the only one who knows I went over to speak to him.'

'I hope for your sake you're right.'

He hesitated, then said, 'I could be a little wrong.'

'I'd say you could be horribly wrong.'

'I can't think how, but they might dig up some reason for wondering if I could have been there. If I can satisfy them that's impossible, that'll end the possibility.'

'How do you propose proving the false negative?'

'If necessary, will you tell the police I was with you for most of the evening? Serena will confirm the story because I said you'd asked me over to offer some advice. It's odds on you'll never be asked to say anything.'

'How many times have you told me you never gamble because you're so hopeless at it?'

'You won't do that?'

'Considering the past, I suppose it's only one more step for a woman. But let's get things straight, if you've an ounce of sense left, you'll tell them the truth just as soon as possible.'

Six

D C Boyne was enthusiastic and imaginatively ener-
getic and therefore one more trial to bear in the eyes
of the detective inspector, who disliked being reminded of
the kind of man he might have been.

Boyne banged on the front door of No. 12 and the
elderly PC opened it. 'About bleeding time!'

'Been feeling lonely?' Boyne asked.

'Been wondering if I was going to have to do the next
turn as well as me own.'

'Wonder on – I'm not here to relieve you.' He stepped
into the hall. 'It seems someone's reported finding what
might be a shirt collar?'

'It is a shirt collar.'

'Why so certain?'

'I've got eyes.'

'So I'll have a butcher's and tell you if your sight's
twenty-twenty.'

'You lot don't dislike yourselves, do you?'

'Never have cause . . . Where is it?'

'Where it was.'

'So lead on, Macduff, and show me.'

'Lay on. Don't they teach you nothing?' The PC led the
way into the kitchen, pointed at the right-hand side of a
wooden-faced unit with marble working surface; the piece
of shaped material lay partly under the door, which had a
two-inch overhang of the base.

Boyne hunkered down; the brief visual examination was sufficient to agree the identification of the curving material, which had a light check pattern in green and red. He picked the collar up. There were many broken threads trailing from the inside edge where it had been torn away from the neck of the shirt; in a couple of places, the material had frayed through from use; there was a small dirt stain near one point. 'Whoever was wearing this must have looked like a tramp. Maybe he was a tramp . . . We'll need confirmation that the deceased's shirt collar was intact.'

'I'm telling you it was.'

'Sure. I suppose you've looked to see if the torn shirt's anywhere around?'

'It's not here in the kitchen. I've had a very quick butcher's over the rest of the place, but I've not done anything more; if I had, like as not you'd be shouting I'd messed everything up.'

'Then I'll make a search.'

He climbed the stairs, which led up from the far corner of the hall, and went into the first bedroom, which from its size and signs of occupation he judged to be the Tobins', a judgement confirmed in the en-suite bathroom where there were toothbrushes in a holder, a tube of toothpaste to the left of the basin and further evidence of very recent use. An Aladdin basket contained some dirty clothes, but no shirt lacking its collar. He returned to the bedroom, walked over to the large picture window and stared out, over the descending line of rooftops, to the Channel, darkly sullen under the overcast sky. Relatively close inshore steamed a large container ship, her appearance made cumbersome by her deck cargo. When young, he'd wanted to go to sea, but his father had dissuaded him. He who would willingly go to sea would visit hell for pleasure; the navy? – rum, lash, and nasty habits. (It was some time before he understood what those habits were.) The sight of a ship bound for some distant, no doubt exotic shore momentarily made him regret his father's influence.

He resumed his search. In the larger built-in cupboard were over two dozen dresses, drawers were filled with underclothes of very good quality, a shoe rack contained twenty-one pairs of shoes, on the dressing table was a set of silver-backed hair brushes, hand mirror, and comb, by the comb was a ring with a single stone which, if the diamond was what it appeared to be, was approaching Ferrari country. It was very strange to meet such signs of wealth in a copper's home, but then Tobin had married the daughter of a rich family, the lucky sod. Except he was dead. Or maybe that was when a man finally did strike lucky.

There was no collarless shirt in any of the other three bedrooms, one of which also had an en-suite bathroom, and he found nothing else of any interest. He went downstairs and, hearing the sound of voices, into the sitting room. The PC was watching television, a half-filled glass on the small table by his side. He noticed Boyle's interest in the glass. 'It's not doing no one any harm,' he said defensively.

Boyle shrugged his shoulders.

'There's enough booze in the larder to keep an army happy. So pour yourself a glassful.'

'I don't reckon.' A senior officer would call it theft.

'Suit yourself,' the PC muttered with uneasy bad temper.

'I'll be off.'

'What about me? When's my relief turning up?'

'Ask your skipper.'

Boyle made his way outside, settled in the car, and

for the first time understood he'd made a mistake when, instead of parking on the road, he'd driven down to the front door. Without the advantage of backing out of the double garage, the available turning area was small; it took him four locks before he could line up the car and drive up to the road.

Wyatt poured himself another drink. Alcohol might be a false comforter, but even false comfort was to be preferred to fearful imagination. He was halfway across the kitchen and heading for the sitting room when he heard a car drive in. He put the glass down on a working surface and hurried outside. Serena had parked in front of the left-hand garage and was helping Leo out of the back of the car; Victoria walked around the bonnet.

'Vicky,' he said, searching for words to say and failing because he found difficulty in expressing emotion.

She hugged him, something she had not done in years. He knew impotent hatred for a world which could offer such pain. Victoria had never enjoyed classical beauty, but her lively, impish, at times rebellious nature was normally reflected in her features, adding character and an intriguing charm. With eyelids puffy, eyes reddened, mouth slack, body slumped, dressed with even less care than usual, she looked plain and lost.

Serena, hand-in-hand with Leo, crossed towards the nearer back door. He watched Victoria follow them. Since the memory of the circumstances in which she'd fled a drunken husband must cause her mental agony, by how much would that be exacerbated should she ever learn his part in what had happened?

By late afternoon, Leo had become fractious through boredom and Victoria asked to borrow her mother's car and take him for a drive. As Serena and Wyatt stood in the yard and watched the Astra draw out on to the road, he said: 'You obviously don't think she might not be in a fit state to drive?'

'She'll be all right. She's a chip off the old block – meaning you.' She tucked her arm around his.

'That's more a liability than an asset.'

'Why do you so often denigrate yourself?'

'Because I know me.'

'You very obviously don't know you. She has the strength to face up to things and accept them as they are, not uselessly wishing they were different.'

'You think I can do that?'

'I know you do do that.'

Two people could live together for many, many years and yet be totally mistaken about the other.

'Why are you looking . . . Well, almost angry? What are you thinking?' she asked.

'That the husband who lives up to his wife's judgement is either a saint or a successful liar.'

'I hate it when you say things like that . . . Let's go in and have tea.' She pressed his arm briefly in a gesture of affection, then released hers and briskly walked across to the nearer doorway.

In the kitchen, she began to fill the base of the coffee machine with water.

'When you told Vicky Frank was dead, did she . . .' He came to a stop.

She looked up. 'Did she what?' The container overflowed and she turned off the tap, emptied out the excess water.

'How did she take it?'

'As you'd expect,' she answered. She began to fill the container with ground coffee. 'She was terribly shocked, but didn't really show it. In a way, it must have helped to have Leo there since she had to try not to upset him too much.'

He rephrased the question. 'Did she talk about Frank on the drive over here?'

'She hardly spoke at all and I was quiet because that's what she obviously wanted; Leo made all the noise. In the next few days she'll probably want to talk and then hopefully it will help her to do so.'

'She didn't explain why she was staying with Hilary?'

'Of course not. You really think she'd bother to do that at such a time?'

'I thought it possible.'

'Simon, she's having to force herself to accept Frank's dead and to ease Leo into understanding that he won't see his father again – everything else is unimportant.'

Then perhaps Serena never would learn that before his death, Tobin had drunkenly struck both Victoria and Leo.

On Thursday afternoon, as daylight was giving way to dusk, Wyatt drove to the mortuary in Setonhurst. There, in the ante-room, in order to provide 'continuity of evidence', he identified Tobin's corpse. Having dreaded the task, he was surprised to find himself relatively unmoved.

The PM room was some thirty feet long, twenty feet wide, windowless, and lit by two overhead pods strong enough to worry weak eyesight. There were three slightly inclined stainless-steel slabs, each with a plughole at the lower end. Two were occupied, one by a young child, the other by Tobin, the bodies propped up slightly by wooden blocks which threw their heads backwards. The skin of the child was yellowish, puffy, and like ancient parchment; that of Tobin still possessed an appearance of life.

Photographs were taken, then McColl, the pathologist, stepped up to the right-hand slab. With no clear idea why this should be, the green gown, surgical gloves, and wellington boots, allied to McColl's aquiline features, recalled to Metcalfe's memory the time he and two pals had skived off school and watched a horror film at the local cinema – he could recall nothing about the film . . .

McColl visually examined the naked body, dictating as he did so. He intently studied one area of the chest, raising his glasses up on to his forehead and putting his face very close to the flesh, short-sightedness making that the best way of gaining optimum detail. 'There's bruising here,' he said, addressing the others present; he recorded shape, size, and exact position of the bruises. More photographs were taken.

He slowly examined the rest of the body as his assistant waited, ready to hand whatever instrument was demanded. When he reached the right hand, he once more raised his glasses and, eyes only inches from the flesh, intently studied the knuckles. 'There are abrasions.' He called for a ruler and laid this, as best he could, against the knuckles so that the scale would be evident in the photographs.

Incisions were made. The years had not inured Metcalfe to the sounds or smells that were released and he tried to lose the present, but failed, as he always did. Blood samples were taken and handed to him as acting lab liaison officer (acting, since this was still listed as an accident); the electric saw made a screeching noise that could bring a man out in a cold sweat. Chest and abdominal organs were lifted out, examined, and dissected on a separate table with running water.

McColl said he was finished and the body could be reconstructed – something that would be done by his assistant so skilfully that when completed it would be almost impossible, without a close examination, to know that both head and body had at one stage been emptied. He stripped off surgical gloves and dropped them into a container for disposal, removed cap and gown and put them in a second one for cleaning, crossed to the far side of the room where he removed his wellington boots and put on a pair of shoes and his coat, both of which had been held in a cupboard whose single door shut so securely against a seal that obnoxious smells could not reach inside.

Some pathologists had an informal manner, McColl did not. He walked through to the ante-room without a word to Metcalfe who followed, lit a herbal cigarette which was almost as offensive to others as the smells he had just left, and paced the twelve-foot-long room. After a while, he said, speaking abruptly: 'The deceased did not suffer a heart attack.'

'Not?' Metcalfe said, mistakenly allowing his surprise to show.

McColl came to a stop and looked at Metcalfe over the tops of his glasses. 'You wish to disagree with my judgement?'

'Of course not, sir. It's just that in the circumstances, that did seem very likely.'

'Preconception is as dangerous as misconception.' He drew on the cigarette, exhaled.

The smoke smelled like silage waste, Metcalfe decided.

'He was a man who clearly ate unwisely, drank immoderately, and took little useful exercise.'

Otherwise, he led a healthy life.

'The injury to his skull was far more serious than an external examination suggested. The skull was fractured and the membrane torn, causing internal bleeding. That his body was found in the hall when it is presumed the injury was occasioned in the kitchen – comparison tests of bloodstains on the table will verify the presumption –

does not necessarily raise any problems. After such an injury, there can be a latent period. Blood accumulates, but the patient appears to be no more than slightly dazed and can indulge in further activities, such as drinking and moving about. Then, usually due to some form of stress, he collapses and dies.

'There is light bruising, which has taken time to appear, on the chest and abrasions on two of the knuckles of the right hand. The bruising is beneath the skin, connecting tissues are not badly crushed, and only a small vein was torn. The abrasions bear no foreign traces, but there is the shadow of a pattern – impossible to photograph – which suggests contact with some form of material. The probability has to be that the deceased both delivered and suffered blows of no great force.'

'He was in a fight?'

'You do not consider that a reasonable conclusion to reach?'

'Yes, but . . .'

'Well?'

'Nothing, sir. Then it's possible that because of the fight, he fell and hit his head on the table?'

'I can give no indication as to the relative timing of the two events.'

'This puts a whole new colour on the case.'

McColl's cigarette had gone out and he brought a box of matches from his trouser pocket.

'I'd better get back and pass on the news. Thank you, sir.' Metcalfe hurried out of the room before the foul smoke resumed.

Seven

'Shit!' Horner said concisely and with venom. He tapped on the desk with his fingers. 'I suppose his written report might be a little less definite.'

Hope was a good breakfast, but a lousy supper, Metcalfe thought.

'At the moment, he's telling us to start treating the case as unlawful killing?'

'Subject to confirmation.'

'Just what we needed when we've twice the work we can handle.'

Typically, the detective inspector was worried about the extra work this was going to cause rather than the extra distress it might bring the family.

'Is there any suggestion who he could have been fighting?'

'Nothing's surfaced to date.'

'What's to say he couldn't have been so tight, he simply banged his fist on a wall?'

'We can't be certain he was tight until we get the results of the blood tests . . .'

'You have to get soaked to the skin before you decide it's raining?'

'The pathologist mentioned an indistinct pattern he saw in or about the abrasions; this could have come from material when Tobin might have hit someone.'

'Could have, might have . . . Is he saying it's likely there was a fight, Tobin was knocked over and hit his head on the table?'

'He wasn't prepared to go that far.'

'Of course he bloody wasn't. The only thing his lot are up to is never being definite until it's so obvious a blind man could see it.'

'He did make the point that we'll need the lab to check whether the blood on the table came from Frank.'

'When we need his advice, we'll ask for it . . . Have you taken blood swabs and sent them to the lab?'

'Not yet.'

'Why not?'

'I've hardly had the time . . .'

'A good detective makes time.'

And a bad one sat on his arse and criticized.

'Talk to the wife and see what she's got to say.'

'Tobin's wife?'

'You think I'm talking about the Prime Minister?'

'Isn't it still too soon after the event to worry her unless we've got cast-iron reason for doing so? It's not forty-eight hours since the husband died.'

'You suggest we hold further enquiries until she tells us she's ready to answer questions?'

The detective inspector could be so small-minded, it was difficult to understand how he had even reached his present rank. 'The way I see things, sir, if there was a fight, it's likely the cause will be found in his work rather than his private life. I'd have said it would be better to avoid causing further distress for the family until we can be certain his assailant was not someone he'd troubled in the past and was out to get his own back.'

'Question her to see what she can tell us.'

*   *   *

Memory was ever remiss. It was only as he was slowly approaching Bredgley Hall along the drive flanked by oaks, Metcalfe remembered that on his previous visit Wyatt's manner had briefly been slightly odd and there had been a small plaster on one cheek. Was it possible . . . Ridiculous! Imagination and police detection were often poor bedfellows.

He parked by the side of the raised circular flower bed, did not immediately leave the car. Ahead lay a tricky time. All men were said to be equal, but unless one was a fool, one did not question a duke in the same manner as a dustman (the duke was more likely to be amenable to questioning). Horner should have been conducting this meeting. That he had chickened out of doing so suggested that with his own retirement so close he was being ever more careful to avoid any action which had the potential to reflect sufficiently badly on him to affect his pension.

Metcalfe opened the driving door and stepped out on to the gravel. To look at the house, scarred and beautified by the centuries, was to feel the touch of history. He crossed to the solid front door and banged the knocker. Gwen would have loved to visit the house. He had had no interest in architectural history before he had met her, yet such had been her enthusiasm for the subject that by the time she had died he had been as keen, though far less knowledge-able, as she. She could look at a house and suggest its age, examine details in roof, walls, and floors, and give a more definite and accurate opinion; show her a king or queen beam – he'd forgotten which was which; presum-ably the king had one more support – and she would give chapter and verse of when that style of construction had begun and when it had been supplanted . . .

Enid opened the door. 'It's you again,' she said, with unwelcoming accuracy.

He asked her if Mr or Mrs Wyatt was at home.

She curtly told him to wait in the hall. No one was more socially conscious than an employee in a rich household and he held no standing in her order of precedence.

Wyatt entered the hall. 'Good evening. If memory serves me correctly, you're Detective Constable Metcalfe?'

'Yes, sir.'

'Would you like to come along in here?'

He followed Wyatt into the sitting room, slightly less luxuriously furnished than the drawing room. There was a large flat television set in front of one wall and extensive hi-fi equipment alongside. Several glossy magazines were on a glass-topped table.

'Do have a seat. And may I offer you something to drink?'

'I wouldn't say no to a lager.'

'I won't be a moment.'

He sat as Wyatt left the room. He visually studied the generously carved overmantel and wondered if it was as old as the house. Gwen would have known. He'd tried to persuade her to study for a degree in domestic archaeology with the Open University and she probably would have done had she not become pregnant. Pregnancy had been a time of pain and sickness and their son had lived for little less than a year. After his death, she had lost the drive necessary to undertake serious adult study . . .

Wyatt returned, handed Metcalfe a filled cut-glass tumbler, sat. 'Your good health.' He drank from a flute.

There was, Metcalfe noted, a fresh plaster on the other's cheek. But sitting there, facing a man whose pleasant, friendly manner marked him as a gentleman in the old, and now largely derided sense, it seemed ridiculous to wonder if the covered sore might have been inflicted by Tobin. 'I'm sorry to trouble you like this, but I'm

61

afraid I must now have a word with Mrs Tobin. I rang her home, but she wasn't there, so I thought perhaps she was staying here?'

'A word about what?' Wyatt's voice had become sharper and tighter.

'There are one or two questions I'd like to ask her.'

'You don't think this is a most unfortunate time to trouble her?'

'Yes, sir, as I said before, I know that it is. Unfortunately, I have no option.'

'I don't understand the reason for that.'

'His death may not have been the straightforward accident it first appeared to have been.'

'What suggests it wasn't?'

'I'd rather not be specific.'

'You'll have to be if you are to persuade me to allow you to question my daughter.'

'She is here, then?'

'We are naturally offering her what comfort we can . . . Why do you now think Frank's death was perhaps not an accident?'

'There are certain indications he may have been in a fight.'

'With whom?'

'We've no idea, which is why I must ask your daughter if she can help us.'

'You say "indications". You are not certain?'

'There will have to be more work done and questions asked before we can be sure.'

'It would be more to the point to have such certainty before submitting my daughter to questioning.'

'I'm afraid we can't always act as we should like to.'

'You insist on questioning her?'

'I shall be as brief as possible.'

'I'll ask her if she's willing to speak to you. If she is not, the interview will be left to another day.'

Metcalfe watched Wyatt leave the room. In a polite, oblique way, he'd been called an unfeeling bastard and if the daughter said stuff him, he'd be stuffed. He stared through the window, which offered another view of the grounds. The gardener was digging a curving flower bed and from the fluency of his actions, the soil was friable despite the recent rain – a far cry from the clay in his small garden at Bankend Street. So much of life was easier for the rich.

Victoria, followed by Wyatt, entered the room.

Metcalfe came to his feet. 'I must apologize, Mrs Tobin, for this, but I have—'

Wyatt interrupted him. 'I explained the situation and my daughter has made the decision to help if she possibly can.'

'It is very kind of her.'

Years had been added to her appearance since he'd last seen her, perhaps three months previously. She opened a chased silver box, brought out a cigarette, picked up a lighter and lit it.

'May I offer you a cigarette?' Wyatt asked.

'Thank you, but I gave up smoking some time ago.'

She said abruptly, her tone harsh: 'Do you know why I'm talking to you?'

Before Metcalfe could answer, Wyatt said: 'Don't you think . . .'

'No.' She drew on the cigarette. 'It's because that's what he'd want. Some people didn't understand him . . .' She looked across at her father. 'You didn't.'

'Vicky . . .'

'He came from another age and the other side of the tracks, so you simply didn't know how to make the effort,

63

even if you'd wanted to. That's just the way it was, it's not really anyone's fault. I tried to explain it to him, but I don't think he ever . . .' She stopped, swallowed heavily. A moment later, she continued speaking. 'He was a policeman because he wanted to help people. He thought that was the most rewarding thing anyone could do. And I'm proud of him because that's how he was. When everyone else rushed around looking after number one, he worried about others, not himself. He once told me the greatest pleasure he enjoyed was when he helped someone who'd become frightened by life and he managed to help them become less fearful. That's the kind of father Leo has . . . had . . .' She began to cry.

'We'll finish this now,' Wyatt snapped.

'No, we won't,' she countered. 'I said, I'm here because that's what he would want.' She brushed the tears from her cheeks, turned to face Metcalfe. 'Well?'

She was a fighter, he thought admiringly. 'I don't know if Mr Wyatt has explained there's reason to think there may have been someone else present in your house on Tuesday night?'

'Yes.'

'And that there may have been a fight?'

'Yes.'

'Have you any idea who that other person might be?'

'No.'

'Do you know if your husband was expecting anyone to call at your house that evening?'

'I don't.'

'Had he recently told you he'd seen or spoken to someone and either he didn't name that person or the name he mentioned was not one you recognized?'

'No.'

'As far as you know, had he recently been worried about something which had happened at work?'

'No.'

'He hadn't returned home and mentioned he'd been threatened or had an unusually strong argument with someone?'

'No.'

'Did he discuss his work with you?'

'Sometimes.'

'If he'd met some sort of trouble, would you have expected him to have mentioned this to you?'

'I . . . I don't really know.'

There were other questions he could have asked, but it seemed to Metcalfe unlikely they'd elicit any relevant information and therefore for her sake it was best to end the interview. 'There's no need to bother you any further, Mrs Tobin. Thank you very much for your help.'

'It's what Frank would have wanted,' she said fiercely. 'When Leo's old enough to understand properly, I'll tell him why he has to be so very proud of his father.'

Metcalfe stood. 'Anyone in the force will underline your words.' Hypocrisy could be a virtue as well as a vice. He said good night to her and left. Wyatt followed him to the front door.

'I judge you hardly learned enough to warrant that ordeal,' Wyatt said.

'As I tried to explain, sir, we often have to do something we would much rather not.'

'What happens now?'

'We make further general enquiries and perhaps more specific ones.'

'If it's confirmed there was a fight?'

'Or there is further evidence to suggest that was very likely.'

'Do you think it will prove to be?'

'I've no way of knowing, but hopefully the pathologist will be able to be more certain later on.'

'If you are continuing your enquiries, you might find my sister may be able to help you in some small way.'

'How would that be?'

'She often saw Frank and Victoria; he amused her. I imagine it's just possible he might have mentioned something to her which he didn't to my daughter, especially if he thought Vicky would be worried by hearing it.'

'Thanks for telling me that.'

'The sooner the truth can be determined, the sooner my daughter will be able to accept what's happened.'

Metcalfe said good night, left, and crossed the drive to his car.

Eight

V ictoria was in her bedroom observing, for the first time in years, one of the principles which had regulated her old life – laugh in company, grieve on one's own. Serena, understanding this while disagreeing with the precept, had taken command of Leo and was bathing him, to his loud discontent. Wyatt went through the outside kitchen to the yard, came to a halt when clear of the light spilling out. The sky had been cleared of almost all cloud by the westerly wind and the stars were bright. Once, they had represented eternal continuity, but cosmologists said that every one would burn out and explode or implode because nothing lasted for ever. But, however innocuous, his involvement in Tobin's death must be hidden for ever; for his own sake, certainly, but even more for Victoria's because the truth would destroy the image of Frank Tobin she was presenting. He walked to his right, around the corner of the house, until in deep shadow and there could be no fear of being seen by those inside. As he brought the mobile out of his coat pocket, a vixen screamed in Farley Woods; the love call sounded like a shriek of agony. Love could be painful. The mobile had a small night light and he switched this on, dialled hurriedly, switched it off. Guilt so spurred the imagination, he had conceived the possibility of Serena's looking out of a window, seeing the light, identifying it and wondering why he was using the mobile instead of one of the house phones. In truth, a ridiculous possibility because she was almost certainly still on the other side of the house and even had she been at one of the upstairs windows on this side, the light was not nearly strong enough to enable her to make out what he was doing . . .

'Yes?' said Charlotte, as curt as ever.

'I've just had a detective in the house.'

'Hardly surprising.'

'They think there maybe was a fight.'

After a short pause, she said: 'How very perverse of them!'

'They're not certain, which is why the detective came here to talk to Victoria. He wanted to know if she'd any idea who might have had reason to fight Frank.'

'Did she?'

'No.'

'She didn't refer to you in any way?'

'Why should she? She's no idea I went there on Tuesday evening. Or that I knew Frank had hit her and Leo before she left home.'

'Do the police know he had?'

'How could they?'

'Because she told them.'

'When it would reflect so badly on him? She's struggling to find something to hold on to and that's a husband to admire, not remember with scorn. She told the detective he served in the police because he saw it as his mission to save others.'

'How long is she going to be able to hide the truth from herself?'

'Who can judge – probably even she can't. Or won't.'

'Did you have the sense to tell the detective what happened when you went to Frank's place?'

'That would have meant the detective's knowing Frank had struck her and Leo. I'd have been betraying her.'

'Not if you'd buttonholed the detective when she wasn't around.'

'It wasn't feasible.'

'You're not ready to suffer the humiliation?'

'That's a filthy thing to say.'

'Do I have to use a seven-pound hammer to drive it into your skull that the longer you leave speaking up, the more your silence will look like guilt?'

'He was drunk, we had a scuffle, and that was that. When I left, he was slumped on the floor. Later on, he must have come to his feet, lost his balance, and smashed his head on the table. The fracas had nothing to do with his death.'

'Is it panic that's making you blind? Your "fracas" will in law be a fight. They'll say you landed punches, which – however light in your estimation – left him so unsteady that he fell onto the table. Which makes you directly responsible for his death.'

'That's a ridiculous way of looking at what happened.'

'Since politicians make the law, the law has an infinite capacity to be ridiculous.'

'For God's sake, stop trying to be smart.'

'For God's sake, be smart. You have to tell the police the truth.'

'It's unnecessary.'

'It's essential so that you cover your back. You've the money to hire top lawyers so that if it all ends up in court, they'll persuade everyone you didn't immediately tell the police because you were so shocked, but as soon as the shock wore off, you realized where your duty lay. That'll bend the jury into believing you're so obviously honest, you really did no more than protect yourself as best you could from a drunken assault.'

'He didn't fall because I hit him.'

There was a silence which he broke. 'I gave your name to the detective.'

'Why?'

'He wanted to know if Frank had ever mentioned anyone whom he thought might cause trouble. I suggested he had a word with you because when Frank was with you, he might have named someone.'

'You didn't add that if we met once a year, that was once too often for me and probably for him as well?'

'I said you often saw Frank and liked him a lot because he amused you.'

'I think you need to consult a psychiatrist.'

'Casually mention I was at your place for most of Tuesday evening.'

'Does he suspect you were at Frank's?'

'Not as far as I could judge.'

'Then wait to prove a false alibi until he does. *Qui s'excuse, s'accuse.*'

'If the information comes from you, he won't suspect anything.'

'That depends how smart he is.'

'He's obviously dependable rather than smart . . . You will do that for me, won't you?'

'If I can't make you see sense, I don't see I have much option.'

'I'm more than grateful.'

'And I'm more than a bloody fool.' She cut the connection.

March was said to come in like a lion and go out like a lamb; this year, it had come in like a hyena and showed no signs of going out in any other guise. The sky was a dirty grey, the rain steady, and during the night, the wind had

70

veered round to the north-east and now carried memories of harsh winters.

As Metcalfe ate, he stared through the kitchen window, made bleary by smeared rain. That morning, an unsolicited holiday brochure had arrived by post. It promised sun, sea, sand and (if one imaginatively interpreted the photographs of bikini- or monokini-clad lissom ladies) sex; he burned easily, was not a keen swimmer, hated the feel of sand between his toes, and in the eyes of nubile young women would probably be capable only of snoring when in bed. He finished the last piece of toast, generously covered with marmalade, stood and carried the dirty plate, mug, spoon, and knife over to the washing-up machine; one more meal and he would need to fire it unless he wanted to wash up by hand. He did not want.

He lifted his raincoat off a peg on the old-fashioned stand in the hall – one of the few pieces of furniture from Gwen's old home – and went out through the front doorway to the lean-to garage to the right of the semi-detached house. The Ford Fiesta was reluctant to start, but on the third attempt the engine spluttered into life, finally settling into a regular rhythm. For weeks he had been telling himself he must take the car to the garage for a service. If he did all the things he was going to, there'd be no time to do anything. He backed on to the road. The wife from No. 41, a colourful umbrella held aloft, stepped out of the small front garden on to the pavement; he waved as he passed, was unsurprised when she barely acknowledged his greeting. The general public was very reluctant to become friendly with a policeman who lived in their midst. Reg Carter claimed that was because they all had nasty secrets they feared might be uncovered. A more interesting reason than the true one, the regrettable modern dislike of any kind of authority, even that which was for a person's own protection.

Traffic was heavy and it took him minutes to edge his way onto the so-called inner ring road that circled within the town. It was difficult to remember Setonhurst as it had once been – a sleepy market town that came to life only on Tuesdays when animals, produce, and hucksters filled the market square and the two hotels, each generously granted a single star, served lunches that kept foreigners abroad. Since those days, easy commuting by train or car had brought light industry, administrative and call centres, housing estates, and greatly increased crime; the market had disappeared and three hotels situated on the outskirts each boasted four stars and served expensive meals that made foreigners wish they had stayed abroad.

He turned off the inner ring road and drove to divisional HQ. He parked, crossed to the building, and inside found the lift waiting – an unusually good beginning to the working day.

In the CID general room, Boyne was talking over the phone; he replaced the receiver as Metcalfe hung his wet mackintosh on one of the wall pegs by the notice board.

'The Guv'nor was asking after you a moment ago,' Boyne said.

Metcalfe crossed to his desk to check if any letters, files, or memoranda had been placed on it since the previous day.

'Seemed to think you were late reporting for work.'

'The traffic was bad.'

'When isn't it? You know what he's waiting to tell you?' Boyne spoke in a remarkably good imitation of Horner's slow speech with the odd word slurred. 'Good timekeeping relies on the keeper, not the clock . . . Where does he get such balls?'

'Christmas crackers.'

'Wouldn't have thought he'd go in for such frivolities . . . Were you watching the telly last night?'

'On and off.'

'Did you see that film there's been so much talk about?'

'Which one?'

'Where the couple get down to really doing it.'

'Wishful thinking.'

'I'm telling you, the two of 'em were starkers so if they weren't enjoying themselves, he must have been so frustrated he ended up knotted.'

'Very painful.' Metcalfe left his desk and walked across to the doorway.

'It'll be repeated soon.'

'The frustration.'

'The film.'

He went out into the corridor. The previous month, they'd confiscated a number of imported video tapes and it had surprised no one when Boyne had volunteered to log the incidence of pornographic material in them.

Horner, who'd been reading a letter, looked up. 'You've finally managed to get yourself here, then?'

'The traffic was very heavy, sir.'

'Only the unforeseeable is excusable.'

Metcalfe interrupted a smile just in time.

'Did you find Mrs Tobin and speak to her?'

'She was with the Wyatts at their place. She couldn't help us. Frank hadn't mentioned anyone or anything which had been worrying him.'

Horner began to drum on the desk with his fingers. 'Are the lab reports through?'

'There's hardly been time.'

'You haven't been chasing 'em up?'

'No, sir.'

'Do I have to tell you to do everything? Ask them if we're going to get the results this year or the next.'

'Before I left the Wyatts, he suggested I talked to his sister; he thought she might possibly have learned something from Frank.'

'Did she?'

'I haven't spoken to her yet.'

'You don't think it might be an idea to do so before so much time has passed she's forgotten?'

'I was only given her name yesterday evening. There's hardly been the chance to question her before now.'

'If you arrived on time, you'd have more time to do your job.'

Not even a Christmas cracker could be that puerile, Metcalfe thought.

'Find out if she can help. And have you sounded out your snouts?'

'Not yet.' He waited for the third imbecility.

'Do that as soon as possible.'

Consistently inconsistent. 'Yes, sir.' Metcalfe returned to the general room, now empty, and searched for the dog-eared telephone directory; it was on the floor. He sat at his desk, thumbed through the pages until he found the number, dialled that, vaguely wondered whether Wyatt's sister had never married, had married and kept her maiden name, or had married and divorced.

'Yes?'

'Miss Charlotte Wyatt?'

'Well?'

'My name is Detective Constable Metcalfe.'

'So?'

Her monosyllabic, aggressive manner painted in his mind the picture of an autocratic, long-faced, buck-toothed female who had once been an enthusiastic mixed hockey player. 'I wonder if I can have a word with you?'

'That is a question for you to answer.'

Uncertainly, he said: 'I don't quite understand.'

'You are the only person who can judge whether or not you are capable of talking to me.'

And a school marm to boot! 'If I drive to your house now, Miss Wyatt, will you be in?'

'If I'm not out.'

'Will you be in or out?' he asked, sounding far more patient than he felt.

'Have I been guilty of parking on solid lines?'

'Almost certainly. But that's not why –'

'I have to leave the house at twelve.' She cut the connection.

He replaced the receiver, conscious he'd almost succumbed to the pleasure of being as rude to her as she had been to him. The police were always on a hiding to nothing when dealing with a civilian determined to be obnoxious, either explicitly or implicitly; senior officers, dealing with a complaint from a member of the public, invariably forgot the provocation to which they'd been subjected when of lesser rank.

The southerly drive to Ronefield took him through a countryside of thorn hedges, small fields, copses, woods, and farmhouses, many of which dated back to the seventeenth and eighteenth centuries. By choice, he would have lived in the country, even though town born and bred; perhaps he was motivated by the genes of great-great-grandfather Brian who, so family tradition held, had been a large landowner, married to an heiress, who had gambled and drunk himself and family into penury. Every family history needed a black sheep to compensate for the present.

Ronefield consisted of a T-junction, a pub that special-
ized in real ales, a handful of houses and bungalows, and a
defunct broiler chicken farm, the sheds of which were now
used by a small company which manufactured specialist
medical equipment. He stopped when level with one of
the bungalows to ask a man, who was preparing earth for
planting, where Bray's Cottage was. The other's voice was
so thick with the local burr that Metcalfe had considerable
difficulty in understanding the directions.

He turned right and then left, passed an inexpertly
farmed orchard not yet showing any signs of new growth,
rounded a shallow bend and came to a gateway on which
was a name board, so weathered that some of the letters
were indecipherable. He turned into the drive and parked
in front of the opened door of a shed used as a garage. He
walked along the gravel surface to a small gate which gave
entry into the garden, opened that and continued along the
brick path to the front door. He rang the bell, looked across
the garden, bounded by a low hedge, at the field beyond
which led to woods. A pigeon on the edge of the woods
suddenly took to the air, as if alarmed.

The front door opened and he turned. She had a round
face rather than a long, thin one, her teeth were neat and
level, and she lacked the boisterously hearty appearance
of a female mixed hockey player, but her question was
couched in autocratic tones. 'What do you want?'

'Detective Constable Metcalfe, county CID, Miss Wyatt.'

A small light and dark brown rough-haired dog with
curled tail appeared, looked up at him and started to
bark.

'Shut up, Isser,' she ordered.

Isser barked more energetically.

'Will you shut up or do I have to shove you in the
kitchen?'

76

'It doesn't worry me,' he said, seeing a chance to create a more friendly atmosphere.

'It does me.' She bent down, picked up the dog and disappeared, leaving him standing outside.

The rain was increasing, so he stepped into the hall, triangular in shape because of the outshut and the inside wall, which was beamed. Like her brother, she enjoyed living in the past – although on a lesser scale.

She stepped out of a room at the end of the hall, shut the door behind herself.

'I moved inside . . .' he began.

'So I observe.'

'It's raining more heavily . . .'

'I also observed that.'

To his surprise, she briefly smiled, stripping her curt words of any offence. Her smile infused her face with a warmth which it lacked in repose.

'Hang your mac upon one of the hooks.'

A wooden coat rack had been fixed to the wall and he fixed his mackintosh on one of the pegs. He followed her into a square room with a low, beamed ceiling and an inglenook fireplace.

Her appearance – no make-up, bulky sweater, shapeless black trousers, clumpy shoes – suggested to him that either she did not bother about appearance or else she was aggressively unfeminine – on so short an acquaintance, it was impossible to decide which.

She halted in the centre of the room, her red hair just clearing the centre beam. He came to a stop.

'Do you intend to remain standing?' she finally asked, as she sat.

He settled on the armchair to the right of the fireplace.

'Well?'

'I imagine, Miss Wyatt, you've heard that, tragically,

Mr Tobin was found dead in his house on Wednesday morning?'

'Yes.'

'He died on Tuesday night and there is reason to believe he might have been involved in a fight before he died. We need to confirm or deny that possibility and are talking to anyone who maybe can help us. Which is why I'm here now.'

'What makes you think I know anything about it?'

'Not about the possible fight, of course, but the cause of that. I understand you were very friendly with Frank Tobin?'

'What leads you to such an understanding?'

'Mr Wyatt said you were.'

'My brother is inclined to exaggerate when he feels that he should for the sake of reputation.'

'What exactly does that mean, Miss Wyatt?'

'You don't find it obvious?'

Her tone suggested he was presenting himself as DC Plod. 'I would rather you told me than that I draw conclusions which could so easily be wrong. Were you very friendly with DS Frank Tobin?'

'DS?'

He could not resist saying: 'You don't find that obvious?'

'You realize, do you, that you're failing to fit the mould?'

'What mould?'

'That painted by the media. Detectives are supposed to be either loud-mouthed bullies or small-minded lechers and never to have the wit to be respectfully rude.'

'I'm sorry if you consider me to have been rude.'

'Wouldn't you be sorrier if I didn't?'

It was a conversation to end as abruptly as possible. Rule 7a in the Manual of Procedure. A police officer will at all times be polite, no matter what the provocation. Had

78

Horner been listening, he would by now have become furious. 'Were you very friendly with Detective Sergeant Frank Tobin, your niece's husband?'

'Friendly is a word with many meanings. I have always had a soft spot for Victoria because she had the gumption to live her own life and so I made a point of getting on as well as possible with Frank, even though we saw the world through such different lenses.'

'You're saying that in fact you weren't all that friendly?'

'I'm saying what I said.'

'Did you and Frank often talk about his work?'

'I tried to avoid the subject because it was my impression that he so often spoke to impress one in regard to his abilities.'

She'd judged him accurately! 'Despite that, has he recently mentioned any circumstances that worried him?'

'I don't remember his doing so.'

'Nothing to suggest he'd been threatened?'

'No.'

'Did he give any indication of being afraid of someone?'

'Not his style to make such an admission.'

'Did he . . .'

There was the sound of scratching on the second door which was behind him.

'How the hell did he escape from the kitchen?' she said, as she stood. 'Ought to change his name to Houdini.' She walked past him and opened the door. Isser bounded into the room, came up to Metcalfe and began to sniff his trousers.

'Come here,' she ordered.

Isser wagged his tail and continued sniffing.

'Don't worry,' he said. 'I like dogs, especially Border terriers.'

'He's a Lakeland . . . Isser, will you come here.'

Isser finally turned away, waited for her to sit and then bounded on to her lap.

'Isser is an unusual name,' he observed.

'It's short for Pisser.'

'Oh!' was all he could find to say.

'He piddles much more than most dogs, but I leave the P off because some people are prudish.'

From the quick look she gave him, she was wondering if he was. 'So Frank never hinted at any trouble which had him worried for his own safety?'

'I think I've already answered that.'

'I'm sorry, Miss Wyatt, but in our job we have to ask the same question more than once.'

'Why?'

'People can sometimes suddenly remember something.'

'Under the spur of irritation?'

'I trust I haven't irritated you too much.'

'Is that a statement or a question?'

'Both, I suppose.' He stood. 'I'll make certain I don't add to whatever irritation I have inflicted and leave.'

'I'm afraid you've had a wasted journey.'

'We get a lot of those. Thanks for your help.' He turned to face the doorway into the hall.

'One moment.'

He turned back.

'Will you be seeing my brother again before tonight?'

'I can't be certain, but I rather doubt it.'

'Then I won't bother you. He left his pen when he was here two or three nights ago – must have been Tuesday evening because he rang me the next morning to tell me about Frank. Had you been seeing him, I'd have asked you to return it to him. He's convinced he can't write properly with anything else. I've suggested a word processor would save him time and trouble since he's forever mislaying the pen, but he's sufficiently old fashioned to be horrified by the idea of printing a private letter rather than laboriously handwriting it. I'm hoping to go to his place this evening and see Victoria and I'll take it to him then.' She edged Isser off her lap and stood. Isser crossed the carpet and sniffed his trousers once more; unexpectedly obeyed the order to come away.

'Do you have a dog?' she asked.

'We had a Schnauzer, but he had to be put down because of old age.'

'You've not replaced him?'

'My wife died not long afterwards and so another dog would have had to be left in the house on its own far too often and for far too long. That's not a fair life.'

'Quite right,' she said approvingly.

He crossed to the doorway and went through to the hall, lifted his mackintosh off the coat rack, gripped the handle of the front door.

From the inner doorway, she said: 'If I'm sufficiently irritated to remember something Frank told me which you might find interesting, how do I get in touch with you?'

'If you'd phone the police station.'

'A number would help me do that.'

'Five six one two . . .'

'I have a sieve for a memory. Wait a minute.' She disappeared, quickly reappeared, small notebook in one hand, pencil in the other. 'Five six one two . . .'

He gave her the number of the direct line into the CID General Room, largely used by informers who would not want to be seen dialling the usual station number. He thanked her once more, said goodbye.

Outside, the rain had begun to ease, but the wind had increased and his unbuttoned mackintosh flapped as he hurried to the parked car. He settled behind the wheel, started the engine, activated the wipers, backed, drove out on to the road.

He'd conducted countless interviews, but could remember none that matched the one just completed. As he turned right, he wondered if her manner indicated she was a lesbian.

Wyatt said over the phone, his tone both angry and uneasy, 'Why weren't you a damned sight more direct?'

'Because that might have made him wonder why I was being so specific; it could have aroused his suspicions,' Charlotte answered.

'Only if he were really smart. He isn't.'

'You can be a bad judge of character, Simon, especially when you're worried.'

'You're saying he's a second Sherlock Holmes?'

'Under that middle-aged, apparently placid exterior, I reckon there's someone a lot sharper than you would like.'

'And I reckon that by the time he drove off, because you didn't underline the facts he'll have forgotten what you said about my being at your place on Tuesday.'

'Facts?'

'You know what I mean. You should have told him I was there the whole evening.'

'Which is what I will if he decides he needs to ask me.'

'It would have been much better . . .'

'Go on panicking like this and you'll give yourself away.'

'I am not panicking. I just wish you'd done as I asked.'

'One day you're going to be bloody glad I didn't,' she snapped.

Nine

Horner fiddled with a spot on the side of his thick neck. 'That's no help.'

'None at all,' Metcalfe agreed.

'But Wyatt said she'd give us useful information.'

How much easier life would be, Metcalfe thought, if people would only act as others said they would.

'Is there any news yet from the lab?'

'They've promised to be in touch as soon as they've any info.'

'If they had to do a full day's work, they'd collapse . . . Have you spoken to the neighbours, prodded the snouts?'

'Not yet.'

'They seem to be the only two words you know.'

'It would make things much quicker if someone else joined in with me.'

'You think I can detail someone with the work load I've got right now?'

Which would become less if he bestirred himself occasionally. Retirement was not supposed to start until one retired.

Horner finally left the spot on his neck alone. 'Get on to the lab again and tell 'em we must have some results, pronto. Question the neighbours. Chase your snouts. Start providing some results.'

Back in the CID room, Metcalfe phoned the forensic

83

laboratory and asked them if they'd any information to offer him. He was told that he might have time to sit around and make unnecessary phone calls, but they had twice as much work as they could cope with and so would he stop bloody bothering them.

The singer might change, but never the song.

Metcalfe braked to a stop on the front, just before the turning which would take him up the short, steep climb to Athin Road. The sea was a sullen grey streaked by small white horses; the horizon was ill defined; inland, the rain had ceased, but out at sea a dark curtain to the west showed where it was still falling. The attractions promised by that holiday brochure became so great that he wondered if he couldn't find a way to avoid sunburn, keep to shallow water, ignore sand between his toes, and meet a woman who did not think him beyond both desire and execution? He sighed. For him, reality never stayed sufficiently far away.

He drove up the sharply rising road to Athin Road. The houses were large and since those on the left were on higher ground than those on the right, all had a good view of the Channel. Estate agents referred to them as individually designed and luxuriously appointed – words worth an extra percentage on the asking prices. Soon after he'd joined the force, he'd been called to one of these houses, where there'd been a burglary. He'd been so impressed by the situation, he'd promised himself that one day he'd live somewhere along the road. Youth was a time of absurd day-dreams.

He stopped in front of No. 12, visually judged the turning circle available in front of the house, left the car on the road. He walked down, rang the bell. There was no response and both front and back doors were locked, proving the police guard had been withdrawn. He returned to the road and made his way to the next house.

The front door was opened by an elderly woman, heavily made-up and dressed in a manner which might have appeared vaguely stylish had she been much younger and more shapely. She briefly studied him, then said in tones which placed a social distance between them: 'Yes?'

'Detective Constable Metcalfe, county CID. You would be Mrs . . . ?'

'What do you want?'

'To ask you to be kind enough to answer a few questions. We're making inquiries following the unfortunate death of Mr Tobin . . .'

'Wait.' She shut the door.

The epitome of politeness.

The door was opened by a grey-haired man who looked as if he found life grim and very earnest. 'My wife tells me you're making enquiries?'

'That's right, Mr . . . ?'

'. . . de Seal. It's about our next-door neighbour? You'd better come on in.'

He stepped into a hall in which hat and coat stand, ornately framed circular mirrors with gilt candle holders, reproduction draw table, telephone table, long-case clock, two wainscot chairs (reproduction), supposedly artistic- ally arranged bulrushes in one polished brass container and pampas-grass in another, left no room for careless movement.

'Come on through, Constable.'

He followed de Seal into the sitting room, which overlooked the sea; it offered an example of the depths to which taste could, when pressed, descend. On a repro- duction drum table and under a domed glass cover was a reproduction Napoleonic prisoner-of-war bone model of a First Rate ship-of-the-line; in two display cabinets were Dresden figurines made in either Hong Kong or Chongqing; the two silver Pekinese on the very ornate mantelpiece appeared to suffer from constipation; the reproduction mahogany breakfast bookcase was filled with books that were never read; the suite of heavy leather furniture had a funereal air; the Kashan carpet was genuine but looked bogus; the oil painting of Mrs de Seal, in a gilded frame, would have been relegated to the attic by anyone who appreciated beauty.

She was seated in an armchair; she waited to speak until they were in the room. 'Are you thinking of coming in here?'

'Yes, dear,' her husband replied.

'It's not convenient. Margery will soon arrive.'

'I didn't know you were expecting anyone . . .'

'I said at breakfast she would be here so that she can tell us all about her cruise to the West Indies . . . You are quite incapable of remembering anything.'

'Yes, dear . . . By the by, didn't she and Edward go to the East Indies?'

'What is the difference? Find out what this man wants and then see he leaves before she arrives.'

De Seal spoke to Metcalfe. 'What exactly is it you're asking?'

'Since you'll have seen quite a lot of Frank Tobin . . .'

Mrs de Seal spoke forcefully. 'The fact one lives next to someone does not mean that one becomes friendly with that person.'

'My wife,' de Seal began to explain, 'unfortunately found Mr Tobin's manner rather difficult . . .'

'Very rude,' she corrected.

Good for Frank, Metcalfe thought. 'But you'll have spoken to him recently?'

After a pause, de Seal said: 'We had a bit of a chat across the hedge on Monday.'

'I do dislike that sort of suburban behaviour,' she snapped.

'Yes, dear, I know. But when he was arriving back as I was leaving, I couldn't just ignore him, could I?'

'I don't understand why not.'

'I didn't . . . That is, I thought I really ought to have a quick word. To show there was no ill-feeling.'

She made a sound that from a lady of less refinement would have been called a snort of derision.

'Did you speak to him, or see him, on Tuesday?' Metcalfe asked.

'Mr de Seal did not,' she answered. 'Now, since you have asked all the questions—'

Metcalfe interrupted her and spoke to de Seal, deliberately repeating his words. 'Did you speak to him, or see him, on Tuesday?' He was rewarded by her expression of sharp annoyance.

'I'm sure I didn't. I saw Mrs Tobin in the morning and . . .' He hastily corrected what he had been about to say. 'But didn't speak to her.'

'Did you notice if anyone called at their house in the evening on Tuesday?'

'I think there was someone, yes.'

'What makes you say that?'

'There was a car on the road. These houses being low down and there not being much room for turning, a lot of visitors leave their cars up on the road. We'd been out with friends and when we returned, there was a car parked in front of their house.'

'What time would that have been?'

'Not very late.'

'Too late,' she said. 'I tried to make you leave earlier,

but you would keep talking to Bartholomew. One should know when to leave, even from a cocktail party.'

'Yes, dear.'

'Have you any idea what the time was when you returned home?' Metcalfe asked her.

They heard the front-door bell.

'That will be Margery. You can go now.'

'If you'll just tell me—'

'Basil,' she said sharply, interrupting Metcalfe, 'let Margery in. Apologize for me not greeting her, but say we're being bothered by a policeman.'

De Seal hurried out of the room.

'I'll be able to leave more quickly, Mrs de Seal, if you'll tell me what time you think it was when you returned here.'

'We left our friends just after nine; we should have left at eight-thirty at the latest. One should always observe the social conventions. Not, of course, that that is a matter to concern you.'

'How long would it have taken to drive back?'

'A quarter of an hour. I do not let my husband drive quickly.'

'So it would have been roughly twenty past nine . . .'

A thin woman, with pinched features, entered.

Mrs de Seal stood and hurried across to engulf the newcomer in a hug of deep friendship; they pecked each other's cheeks before they parted. 'Sit there, Margery. It's the most comfortable chair, which is why Basil always tries to use it. Men are so selfish . . . Have you brought dozens of photographs of your cruise? I've always wanted to sail the seven seas, but Basil is such a stay-at-home I can hardly persuade him to go anywhere. Of course, one does have to be so careful these days when almost anyone can afford to go on some of the cruises. It quite ruins a holiday when many of the other passengers are . . . You know what.' She briefly looked at Metcalfe.

'I've one last question,' he said, 'then I can leave.'

She ignored him.

'Can you describe the car; colour, type, and make?'

'It was not a Rolls-Royce.'

The only marque she allowed herself to recognize? As he left the room, she was describing how their great friends had gone for a cruise and found their fellow passengers quite . . . Margery knew what.

He was surprised that de Seal followed him into the hall.

'Sorry we couldn't help you any more,' de Seal said.

'Maybe you can.'

'How's that?'

'From what your wife told me, when you returned here on Tuesday evening, it was roughly twenty past nine. Would you agree with that time?'

'If she says that's what it was, then that's what it was. A great stickler for time.' He allowed himself a rare moment of free speech. 'Especially leaving time.'

'Did you notice what make of car it was?'

'Difficult to tell one from another these days. But it definitely was an estate.'

'Did you see the registration number?'

'Can't say I did.'

'What about colour?'

'It could have been green, but it's difficult to judge in street lighting . . . To tell the truth, I thought it looked like her father's car, which is green.'

'What make is his?'

'Can't say I've ever really noticed.'

'Then it's not a Rolls.'

He looked at Metcalfe, then quickly away.

'We can find out easily enough. Thanks for your help.'

'Glad to do what we can.'

Metcalfe left and walked up to the road, then along to the house on the other side of No. 12 – a bungalow built in a U-shape. He spoke to a young, smartly dressed and attractive woman who proved to be talkative. She and Garry – her husband – were friendly with the Tobins and the news of Frank's death had been a nasty shock. They'd had drinks at their house on Sunday morning. Frank had drunk rather more champagne than he should have done, a not uncommon occurrence. Garry often wished he'd the money the Tobins spent on drink because he'd buy . . .

Metcalfe returned the conversation back to the matter in hand.

Frank had not recently mentioned anything that was bothering him – apart from senior officers – or anybody who'd threatened him. She hadn't seen the car parked outside the Tobins' house on Tuesday evening because although she and Garry had intended to go out, the baby sitter had called off and they'd had to stay at home. She thought Mr Wyatt drove a Volvo estate.

Metcalfe returned to his car and settled behind the wheel, but did not immediately drive off. He recalled the manner in which Wyatt had exclaimed 'Impossible!' when told of Tobin's death – almost as if he'd had reason to believe that was so, rather than using the word in the context of instinctively, futilely denying death could be so randomly cruel.

Ten

It was seven that evening before Metcalfe finished the more pressing paperwork. The bureaucratic necessity to fill in forms on every and any occasion had become the curse of a detective's life – to the extent that when there was possible doubt, a suspect might be released rather than face the thirty-one forms the arrest could demand.

From the far side of the room, Jamieson, on night duty, said: 'Have you had anything to do with the Guv'nor since lunch time? Someone's stuck a wasps' nest up his breeches. Had me in his room and tore a strip off me for no reason.'

'That's called the privilege of rank.'

'Any idea what's made him so bloody bad-tempered?'

'He's probably discovered CID is already overspent for the month.' Horner, as had he, had joined the force when results were more important than the balance sheets. Since then, successive governments had reversed the priorities to the detriment of everyone. Old hands were not accountants and forward financial planning remained an unknowable mystery . . .

'You're lucky to be getting out of it all. Just how long have you to go?'

'A little over a couple of months.'

'That's about as long as the Guv'nor, isn't it?'

'So someone said.'

'I wonder who'll move in?'

'There's talk it could be George Acton.'

'What are the rumours about him?'

'A go-doer. Which will make a change.'

'For the worse, like as not.'

'Change always is for the worse.'

'You know something? You can be a miserable bastard!'

'That's what keeps me sleeping happy.'

Metcalfe left, walked along the corridor past the empty rooms of the detective inspector and detective sergeant, pressed the button to bring the lift up to the fifth floor. Sleeping happy? Sometimes his sleep was bitter because he dreamed he and Gwen were still together.

He left the building and crossed to his car, parked in a bay reserved for the duty inspector because no other had been free when he'd driven in. Pinned against the windscreen by one of the wipers was a handwritten note to the effect that if he parked again in that bay, he'd be hanged, drawn, and quartered, then disciplined. He scrumpled up the paper and aimed it at a litter basket, missed, picked it up off the tarmac and dropped it in. He opened the car door and settled behind the wheel. Miss Wyatt's statement. Should he or shouldn't he bother to ask her to confirm what she'd mentioned to him? She struck him as someone who seldom needed to confirm herself, but it had been said so casually her mind might not have been wholly on her words. An interesting person because she was so different . . .

He drove out of the car park and turned left, heading for Ronefield. He might be on the verge of retirement, but he still wanted to do the job to the best of his ability . . . Yet that need to accept the truth that plagued him made him admit that in part his decision had been made because he looked forward to meeting her again. As he braked for lights, he asked himself, Why? Her direct manner frequently suggested antagonism, she was no beauty, probably was an aggressive feminist . . .

Twilight was about to become dark and as he drove through the countryside, the headlights carved a way between the hedges on either side; from time to time, they picked out the crouching form of a rabbit, ears laid right back, momentarily frozen by fear, then self-preservation became stronger and it fled to the black safety.

As he approached the village, he decided he was a bloody fool, wasting his own time, not the police's; as he turned right at the cross-roads, he wondered whether to abort the journey and return home . . .

He braked to a halt in the drive of Bray's Cottage, left the car and walked round to the front door, across which the curtain had been drawn so that a visitor could not look inside. A sensible security precaution. Common sense was surely one of her fortes? But, he mentally added, in certain circumstances she might well throw common sense to the winds. He rang the bell. Isser began to bark; his enquiring head pushed aside a corner of the curtain and he looked out. An outside light was switched on, the curtain was drawn back.

Charlotte unlocked and opened the front door; Isser, barking, rushed out, circled him once, then ran off to the right and disappeared. She called him several times, without effect. 'The day he does something I tell him to do, I'll reward him with the largest bone the butcher can provide.'

She'd taken more care over her appearance than on the previous occasion he had met her. She wore a colourful jersey over a lace-edged blouse, full skirt, and modest make-up. There was a touch of feminine softness. He doubted she would feel flattered if told that. 'I don't think he's ever going to enjoy that treat,' he said.

'I'd bet a small fortune he won't . . . Come on in. It's not raining, then?'

'The sky's almost clear.' He stepped into the hall as she continued to call. Eventually, Isser appeared.

She sniffed. 'Has he rolled in something or is he just announcing he's here?' She picked him up and held his wriggling body for a short while, replaced him on the floor. 'False alarm. The trouble is, sometimes he finds a cow's or horse's offering, rolls in it, and comes back delighted with himself. I don't know which is worse. Which would you say?'

'I don't think I've ever had occasion to decide.'

'A typical male – always leave the woman to do the dirty work. I'll bet you never changed a nappy.'

'Wrong.'

'How many children do you have?'

'Our only child died very young.'

'I'm sorry to have splashed in sad waters.'

'It's a long time ago,' he said dismissively.

She hesitated, then spoke briskly. 'Are you going to be here long enough to enjoy a drink? If so, what would you like?'

'Can I have a gin and tonic?'

'You may and can, provided I remembered to buy more tonic the last time I shopped.'

He'd forgotten that touch of school marm.

'Go on in and sit and I'll bring the drinks along.'

He went into the sitting room and settled on the far side of the fireplace. There was a small log fire in the fire basket, behind which was a fireback dated 1673, and as he stared at the advancing and retreating flames, he wondered if her direct manner was her way of keeping men at bay . . . He silently swore. Because his job had taught him to search for what was hidden, he was forever assuming that something was.

She returned, a silver salver in her right hand, Isser by her side. She handed him one glass, put the salver down on a small table by the side of the other fireplace chair, sat; Isser jumped on to her lap. 'Is this a social visit or the call of duty?'

He assumed there was light mockery in her words. 'Suppose I answer it's a combination, with the former predominating?'

'A case of flattery soothing the dull cold ear?'

'Far from it,' was his weak reply.

She drank. 'It's not really cold enough for a fire, but I lit one for cheerfulness, a valuable commodity when one's on one's own. I gather from something you said before, you find that?'

'All too often.'

She fondled Isser's ear. 'Suppose we get the call of duty out of the way so we can relax?'

'I'd like to ask a few questions.'

'Which are?'

'Can you be quite certain it was Tuesday evening when Mr Wyatt was here with you?'

She stopped petting Isser, picked up her glass drank, lowered the glass, said: 'Do you have a very poor memory?'

'I've always hoped it's average.'

'Then you're setting out to irritate me?'

'Why d'you suggest that?'

'You told me you ask the same questions over and over again in the hopes that under the spur of irritation, your victim will remember something more.'

'I'm sorry you seem to think of yourself as a victim. All I'm seeking is confirmation.'

'You believe I was lying?'

'Of course not.'

'If you accept I was telling the truth, there should be no need for confirmation.'

'I'm not allowed to employ common sense. My senior officer won't accept anything until it's been confirmed half a dozen times. Tell him it's night and he'll demand proof the sun isn't shining.'

'It seems to me you're trying to cover yourself at my expense.'

'I suppose one could look at it in that light.'

'I can and do. But I'll be generous. Yes, I am quite certain.'

'Why?'

'It happened only four days ago and, as I remember telling you, he was here in the evening before we heard about Frank's death.'

'When did Mr Wyatt arrive?'

'In the early evening.'

'Can you put a time to that?'

'No.'

'When did he leave?'

'Fairly late.'

'It would help a great deal if you could be more definite.'

'Why?'

'It would prove beyond all doubt that Mr Wyatt was here when Frank Tobin died.'

'Are you making the insulting inference that my brother could in any way be connected with Frank's death?'

'I'm inferring nothing. But I have to make certain Mr Wyatt was here because evidence has come to light that a car was parked outside Frank's house at the relevant time and it's been suggested it was Mr Wyatt's—'

She interrupted him. 'Despite all your soft words, you are calling me a liar and suggesting my brother did have something to do with Frank's death.'

'If you'd given me time, I'd have explained that what I'm trying to do is prove it could not have been your brother's car even if the one that was seen was the same make, colour, and model.'

She spoke more calmly. 'You've an odd way of doing that.'

'Then I apologize for being so ham-fisted.'

'Or deliberately provocative in the hopes of learning something more?'

'That would be to credit me with far more subtlety than I possess.'

She picked up her glass and drained it. 'My brother was here on Tuesday evening and he left relatively late, which means it probably wasn't all that short of midnight.'

'Then the car in question couldn't possibly have been his.'

'You're finally beginning to believe me?'

'I believed you from the beginning. Now my detective inspector will have to do the same.'

'Does that mean you don't intend to ask any more insulting questions?'

'That is the end of the Inquisition.'

'Then maybe we can move on and enjoy the social side of your call. I'll pour another drink.' As she began to move, Isser jumped down on to the floor, crossed to Metcalfe, jumped on his lap.

'I hope you'll realize the great honour you've just been granted,' she said. 'It's not everyone he'll be so friendly with.'

97

'I must smell right.'

'I think it safer to make no comment.' She crossed to his chair. 'Give me your glass . . . Tim used to say that I drowned the gin, so did I pour too much tonic the first time?'

'It was just right,' he answered, as he held up his glass.

'I never really accepted his criticism because it was one of his misguided beliefs that no woman could mix a decent drink.'

'Tim was your husband?'

'In modern parlance, my partner.' Her tone briefly became bitter. 'Unfortunately, partnerships break up as easily as marriages.' She turned on her heels and left.

He stroked Isser's head. So much for his perverse imagination. He hoped she had gained no inkling of the realms into which his thoughts had strayed.

She returned, handed him his glass, sat. Isser deserted him, went across and jumped onto her lap, causing her to jerk her glass and spill a little of the white wine on to her skirt. 'Beastly little dog,' she said affectionately, as she brushed away as much liquid as possible with her hand.

There was a brief silence, which she broke. 'I usually have supper around eight . . . Well I'll be damned! I've just remembered Simon arrived here on Tuesday as I started eating. I offered him food and he said he wasn't hungry, then polished off a plateful of cold ham and salad.'

'You're now saying he arrived here some time around eight?'

'Since nothing happened to change my routine, yes, I am.'

'Remembered without the spur of irritation!'

'Which you must find very irritating!'

He smiled, looked up at the carriage clock on the top shelf of the small alcove to the right of the fireplace. 'It's already well after eight so I'm upsetting your routine.'

'If my routine were that inviolable, I wouldn't have offered you a second drink.'

'Nevertheless, I'll try not to delay your meal much longer.'

'It does one good voluntarily to alter one's habits. Why not alter yours and have supper here? I usually have cold meat, salad, and cheese, but I could make an omelette or defrost a couple of lamb chops if you'd like something more solid?'

'Cold meat and salad sounds delicious.'

'Good.' She stared down at her glass. 'I think you said your wife had died?'

'Some years ago.'

'So you're on your own?'

'I have been since then.'

'Do you find life very lonely?'

'All the time.'

'Does one ever come to terms with loneliness?'

'Probably only if one's an anchorite.'

'There can't be many of them around in these consumer days.'

A piece of burning wood fell through the bars of the fire basket and a small, waving column of smoke rose into the room. Instinctively, he stood and with the pair of fire tongs, picked it up and replaced it in the basket; then, because the fire had fallen low, he added a couple of small logs taken from the polished copper basket. Only as he once more sat did he realize he might have given the impression of someone making himself so at home he must imagine an invitation to supper included the offer of a shared bed. 'I'm sorry.'

'For what?'

'Acting without being asked.'

'The mark of a thoughtful person.'

He wondered if she was secretly laughing at him.

Wyatt was checking all downstairs doors and windows were secured when the telephone rang. He crossed the kitchen to the receiver fixed on the wall.

'Alec was here this evening, he's just left,' Charlotte said.

'Alec who?'

'The detective who's asking all the questions.'

'What the hell does he think he's doing, calling at your place this late at night? I'll make an official complaint . . .'

'How typical! You'll complain to no one. He arrived earlier and stayed on because I invited him to supper.'

'You did what?'

'Watered and fed the beast.'

'Are you crazy? God Almighty! He's trying to stick his nose into everything and you go out of your way to encourage him.'

'Because I reckoned that in the circumstances, the more honest, pleasant, and friendly at least one of the family appeared to be, the better for you.'

'What circumstances?'

'Someone's reported seeing your car outside Frank's house on Tuesday evening at the vital time.'

He experienced sharp and sudden fear. 'Who says that?' he asked hoarsely.

'He didn't name names, but most likely it was one of the neighbours.'

'Then it'll have been that awful woman who lives next door.'

100

'I said it couldn't have been your car because you'd spent the evening at my place.'

'He believed you?'

'As far as I could judge.'

'What times did you say I was with you?'

'From around eight to not far short of midnight.'

'Why were you so uncertain?'

'In order not to be pinned down and so later proved a liar. In any case, not knowing exactly when Frank died, I'd no idea what was the precise critical time which had to be covered.'

'It would have been better to be more precise.'

'Simon, you're not thinking straight because you're panicking. Your car obviously has not been definitely identified, but there could be more damaging evidence to come and I had to allow for that fact so that I can keep you in the clear. Can't you understand that?'

'Yes, but . . .'

'But me no buts. He'll be along to your place, probably tomorrow morning, to check whether you tell the same story. So remember, you don't know what the time was when you arrived, but I had started my supper. I offered you a bite, you said you weren't hungry and then demolished a meal of cold ham, salad, and cheese. You've no real idea of when you left, but it must have been close to midnight – that has the added benefit of being the truth because that was when you'd calmed down sufficiently to go home. Whatever you do, however much he bullies you, don't give definite times. Was Serena awake when you got home?'

'Yes.'

'And you said goodnight to her?'

'Of course.'

'So she'll back you up.'

'Yes . . . Christ!'

'What?'

'She noticed the shirt I was wearing wasn't one of mine. If the police learn I changed my shirt, they'll want to know why and if I say it had become torn . . .'

'Make certain she doesn't mention it to them.'

'If I tell her to forget the shirt, she'll want to know why and she's so straightforward the police are bound to suspect she's hiding something. She can't conceal a thing.'

'Unlike you.'

'Never lose a chance to get a dig in, do you?'

'You don't think it's warranted when you spend time with some other woman?'

'It's only occasionally.'

'And like the little baby, that makes everything OK?'

'You don't understand.'

'That's in my favour.'

'You can't know what it's like for me.'

'Does anyone ever know what life's like for someone else? . . . What did you tell Serena when she remarked on your shirt?'

'That she'd said to change the old one I had been wearing and it had come out of my cupboard.'

'And she believed you?'

'Yes. What do I do if the police say they want to question her?'

'Which they will, to check she can corroborate your alibi. Since you reckon you daren't ask her to keep quiet, make certain you're there when she's questioned and if there's the slightest chance of her telling the truth, head her off.'

'How?'

'That has to be up to you.'

'It's all become so . . . so impossible.'

'Scott knew a thing or two.'

'Scott?'

'"O what a tangled web we weave, When first we practise to deceive!"'

Eleven

As she poured out the breakfast coffee, Serena said, 'I forgot to mention that Vicky's thinking of spending a few days with Denise.'

'Who's Denise?'

'For goodness' sake! Very soon, you'll be asking me who Vicky is. Denise is one of her oldest friends, who lives up in Cheshire. She was the fluffy blonde bridesmaid who flashed her deep blue eyes at all the men and made them think themselves years younger.' She passed him a cup, began to butter a piece of toast. 'I told her I thought it was a very good idea and to go as soon as she feels up to it. With all Denise's children as well as Leo to cope with, she won't have much time to think of Frank . . . Have you any idea when the police will release his body?'

'No.'

'She wants cremation and only us at the crematorium. She says that that may upset some of his friends, but they'll just have to get over it. And as far as his family is concerned, there are only two cousins and there's been no contact with them since the marriage; in any case, she doesn't want them to be present. Which is hardly surprising. Do you remember how the two families behaved?'

'No.'

'I'm surprised they aren't etched in your memory. At

the time, you said they were the only people you'd ever known who could manage to break every canon of social behaviour in a single afternoon . . . Of course, your cannons are so old fashioned they're easily breached.'

'How's that?'

'An attempted joke which clearly fell flat . . . What's wrong, my sweet?'

'Nothing.'

'Yes, there is. You're living in that other world into which you sometimes disappear. Is it . . . You know?'

He made the effort to forget the probable police interview and be more companionable. 'I keep thinking of Vicky and how her life has suddenly been blasted apart.'

'Between you and me . . . She's still upstairs with Leo, isn't she?'

'As far as I know.'

'I'm hoping that once this tragedy is in the past . . . Judith told me the other day that Roger's separated and probably getting a divorce. His wife said she wanted to start aerobic classes and he's always given her everything she's asked for. She spent more and more time supposedly at the classes and then he discovered she was having an affair with the man who owns the business. I simply can't understand how she could have behaved like that. Can you?'

'No.'

'Of course you can't. How stupid of me to ask!' She had been about to pick up a piece of toast, instead reached across the table and put her hand briefly on his wrist. 'You honour your promises, however terribly difficult that is, because—'

'It's possible the detective will be back, asking more questions,' he said abruptly.

She was plainly hurt by the curt way in which he had

interrupted what she'd wished to say, but accepted he would have been embarrassed by her display of emotion.

'He may want a word with you as well as with me. If so, just answer the direct question, nothing more.'

'I'm not certain what you mean.'

'Don't add details which can't be of the slightest significance or he'll start prying into every part of our lives.'

'What could I tell him that would be of the slightest significance?'

'If the law and the police knew the meaning of logic, there'd be a lot less crime.'

Wyatt was trying to persuade Wade that enlarging one flower bed and narrowing another would provide a greater sense of symmetry to that part of the garden, when a grey Fiesta drove into the yard. As the driver climbed out and he recognized Metcalfe, he suffered a sharp stab of fear even though this was a meeting he had been expecting. 'I'll have to see what he wants . . . We'll talk things over again a little later on.'

'As you like.' A dour character, Wade resented any change made at someone else's suggestion rather than his own. It was 'his' garden.

Wyatt crossed the lawn to the yard where Metcalfe stood by the car. Charlotte repeatedly stressed how important it was to be on friendly terms with the detective – difficult, when one wished him to hell.

'Good morning, Mr Wyatt. Sorry to bother you again, but there's something cropped up that needs sorting out.'

'Then come along inside.'

They went into the sitting room. Wyatt offered coffee or, the morning being well advanced, a drink. Metcalfe declined both.

'I'm here because I've had a word with some of the people living in Athin Road and one of them told me they'd seen a car parked outside Frank Tobin's house at the relevant time on Tuesday evening –'

Wyatt interrupted the other. 'What is the relevant time?'

'We can't be certain when Frank died, but the best evidence is between eight and eleven. Obviously, we need to know whose car that was because although he, or she, may well be unable to help us, we can then eliminate that person from our enquiries. I expect your sister has told you we have a suggested identification of the car?'

To deny she had been in touch with him would raise the presumption he could not have prepared himself to deny the identification; on the other hand, it must seem likely she would have mentioned the detective's visit. 'She rang to tell me what had happened.'

'Then you know it is alleged the car was yours?'

'Yes.'

'Was it yours?'

'No. As my sister tried to make clear to you.'

'As I told her, Mr Wyatt, we often have to make our-selves sound right Charlies by asking the same questions over and over again . . . Moving on, clearly that car was very similar, perhaps identical in appearance with yours, so it'll be valuable to us to know what year, make, and model yours is?'

'A Volvo seventy estate, roughly eighteen months old.'

'Even in these days of lookalikes, that has a fairly distinctive shape so it's very likely the car was a Volvo estate. What colour is yours?'

'Green.'

'The car in question was said to be green, but colour isn't easily determined in street lighting. I think it'll be safer to describe it as of a darkish colour, possibly green . . . Would you now corroborate one or two things your sister told me?'

'Depending on what she said.'

'She didn't explain when she phoned you?'

'She spent almost all the time complaining you'd asked questions she'd already answered a dozen times.'

'I hope that is at least a slight exaggeration! . . . You arrived at her house at what time?'

'I'm not certain.'

'Could you give a rough estimate?'

'I suppose it was around eight.'

'Before or after?'

'It could have been either. My sister had just started supper when I arrived and I joined her. Perhaps she can be more specific.'

'When did you leave?'

'It must have been nearing midnight.'

'Did you leave her house between those times?'

'No.'

'Was there any particular reason for spending the evening with her?'

It was not a question he had expected and it momentarily flummoxed him; then common sense returned and he realized it was easily answered. 'She lives on her own and is naturally lonely, so I like to spend time with her.'

'Of course.'

'Added to which, I try to advise her on certain financial matters.'

'There is one more point to cover before I get out from under your feet. Is Mrs Wyatt at home?'

'Why do you ask?' Wyatt futilely wished his voice hadn't sharpened, possibly making the other wonder why the question had disturbed him . . . But when he surreptitiously studied the detective's expression, he saw no suggestion of sharpened interest.

'She will corroborate much of what you've told me,' Metcalfe answered.

'You think I'm lying?'

'Very far from it, but as I told your sister when she thought the same thing, we have to double- and treble-check everything because the detective inspector wouldn't believe an archangel unless there was corroboration.'

'You want to speak to her to gain the necessary corroboration?'

'That's what I should like, yes.'

'I'll find out if she's free.'

He left the room and carefully closed the door, moved away only slowly. Did he say she'd gone out? Wouldn't he have known she had? If the door of the second garage was open, the detective might have seen her Astra and that would brand him a probable liar. He could say she was ill in bed, but Sod's Law decreed she would come face to face with the detective as he left . . .

She was in the kitchen, lightly frying small pieces of meat. 'The detective's here,' he said.

'I wondered whose car that was. What's he want this time?'

'To have a word with you.'

'For Heaven's sake, why? I can't tell him anything.'

'He'll ask you what time I left and returned on Tuesday night.'

'Haven't you told him?'

'Yes, but his middle name is Thomas and he wants corroboration.'

'I can't suddenly stop cooking the meat and resume later on or it won't be nearly as nice.'

If her attention was on the cooking rather than answering questions, she surely would be less likely to remember the shirt? 'The best thing, then, is to bring him in here.'

'Must you?' She looked around the kitchen. 'It's not very tidy.'

'Probably much tidier than his own place. It'll be the quickest way of getting rid of him.'

'Then if you must.'

He returned to the sitting room. 'My wife's in the middle of cooking and swears she can't possibly break off or the meal will be ruined. Will you talk to her in the kitchen or would you prefer to wait – which could mean quite a long time?'

'If it's all the same, I'd like a word now.'

'Then will you come through?'

As they entered the kitchen, Serena looked up and said good morning; Metcalfe returned the greeting. She apologized for the stained apron she was wearing, he gallantly said what was an apron for if not for spotting; he added that the smell suggested a delicious meal.

She was pleased by his praise. 'We like steak and kidney pie, so I often make it.'

'I have to do my own cooking, so I usually buy readymade food, which isn't the same thing by a long chalk . . . You fry the meat first?'

'Flour it lightly and fry it lightly before cooking in the oven – that makes all the difference. And add lots of mushrooms.'

'I must try that next time I find the energy to cook.'

She moved to the table in the centre, placed a sieve on top of a plastic bowl, returned to the stove and picked up the saucepan, then carefully poured the contents into the sieve to allow the fat to drain away. After returning the saucepan, she opened a pack of ready-made puff pastry and placed two sections on a chopping board.

'Mrs Wyatt, you certainly won't want me cluttering up the place any longer than necessary when you're so busy, so if you'll be kind enough to answer a couple of questions, I'll clear off,' Metcalfe said.

She hurried across to the nearest unit and opened the top drawer, brought out a wooden rolling pin.

'I have to ask you if you can tell me when your husband left here on Tuesday evening?'

She began to roll out the pastry. 'It was fairly early because we hadn't had supper; I had a little later on, but not very much because I was still suffering from the flu.'

'What sort of time would that make it?'

She stopped rolling and looked at Wyatt. 'You'll know better than I; I'm so hopeless about times.'

'I won't argue with that, but I'm sure Mr Metcalfe would prefer you to answer,' Wyatt replied.

'I suppose it was some little time before eight.'

'And when did your husband return?' Metcalfe asked.

'I wasn't asleep because I like to know my husband is safe and sound. I remember looking at the bedside clock when it was half-past eleven and thinking he was rather late; I suppose he returned near midnight. He came up to my room and I asked him if he'd had supper and when he said he hadn't—'

Metcalfe interrupted her. 'He said he hadn't had supper?'

Wyatt mentally struggled to overcome the panic her words had promoted.

'Yes, why?'

Wyatt said hastily: 'I've been caught out, like the underfed guest raiding the fridge . . . I wasn't thinking and had momentarily forgotten I'd had something to eat

111

at Charlotte's, was about to tell you that when you said there was Enid's shepherd's pie to finish. That's always so delicious, I decided to keep quiet and sneak a mouthful without the fear of being reminded my waist isn't getting any smaller.'

'A mouthful! I only had a little and you finished all that was left.'

'*Carpe diem.*'

'How's that, Mr Wyatt?' Metcalfe asked.

'A hymn to the resolve to eat, drink, and be merry.'

'You certainly followed that advice!' she said.

'I have to declare my sympathies,' Metcalfe remarked. 'I've always had room for a good shepherd's pie.'

Wyatt relaxed. Very quick thinking, spurred by temporary panic, had saved the day.

'Mrs Wyatt, you'll be glad to know there's only one more question. On his return home, was there anything unusual about your husband's appearance?'

Avoid the whirlpool and be gobbled up by the female sea monster. Redoubled tension seemed to force the breath out of Wyatt's lungs. His fear had always been that Serena would inadvertently mention the shirt; it had never occurred to him that she might be directly asked about it. Pray to all the gods that her memory proved weak . . .

The inner kitchen door slammed open and Leo, crying, rushed across the kitchen and wrapped his arms around Serena's legs. She held him and asked what was wrong; when he complained bitterly that his mother wouldn't let him eat any chocolate, she explained that chocolate in the morning spoiled lunch. He declared he didn't want any horrible lunch . . .

Metcalfe, a shade impatiently, asked for the second time whether there had been anything unusual about her husband's appearance on his return home that night.

She discovered that flour on her hands had been transferred to Leo's cheek. 'What will your mother say if she sees you looking like a ghost? Come on, we must go to the cloakroom and wash the flour off.' She took Leo's hand and they began to walk towards the inner doorway.

'Please Mrs Wyatt, if you could answer me?' Metcalfe said.

'Of course there wasn't anything unusual,' she answered, just before she and Leo left the kitchen.

'I'll be on my way, then, Mr Wyatt,' Metcalfe said. 'Once again, thanks for all your help.'

'We're happy to do all we can.' Wyatt, taking care to move casually, walked over to the outer door and opened this.

Outside, Metcalfe expressed the hope he would not have to bother them again, said goodbye, climbed into his car and drove out of the courtyard on to the road.

Wyatt, emotionally drained, returned to the kitchen. Serena and Leo entered seconds later. 'Simon, why did the detective ask me if there was anything unusual about your appearance?'

'I've no idea.'

'It seems such an odd question.'

'A meaningless one.'

'The funny thing is, I was fussing over Leo and forgot you'd come back in a strange shirt. Do you think I ought to have told him that?'

'It'll hardly interest him that I found one in my cupboard you didn't recognize.'

'I suppose it can't . . . Someone is becoming bored. Would you like to take him for a walk around the garden?'

'A pleasure.' It would be – a thanks to Leo for being both seen and heard.

Twelve

The door of Horner's room was open and Metcalfe knocked as he entered. 'I'm just back from talking to the Wyatts, sir.'

'Well?'

'She confirms what both her husband and Miss Wyatt have said.'

'Then it wasn't Wyatt's car outside Tobin's house.'

'Not according to their evidence.'

'Any reason for doubting that?'

'Not exactly. But there was one oddity. Miss Wyatt had told me he had had supper at her place the night Frank died. Mrs Wyatt said that when he returned home, well after eleven-thirty, she asked if he'd eaten and he replied not, so she told him to finish a shepherd's pie which he did.'

'How did he explain the inconsistency?'

'With some sort of Latin phrase and the fact that he likes shepherd's pie so much, he tucked in despite the previous meal.'

'Sounds possible.'

'He didn't make it sound all that believable and his body language suggested that if things became any tighter, he'd need a change of underclothes.'

'And?'

'That's it.'

114

'Not exactly conclusive.'

'I know, but I've the feeling we're a long way from the truth.'

'Feelings aren't any use in a witness box. Restrict yourself to facts . . . Have you been on to the coroner's officer again to ask if they're ever going to provide the PM report?'

'He's promised he'll be in touch the moment he hears from the pathologist.'

'A promise not worth a tinker's spit . . . Have any of your snouts come up with useful info?'

To say there still had not been the time to question any of them would be to exacerbate the detective inspector's bilious mood. 'My best possibility can't help off the cuff, but will lengthen his ears. I'll be talking to the others when I can find them.'

'So how do things look right now?'

'Our only useful lead seems to be the car outside Frank's place, which apparently couldn't have been Mr Wyatt's. Since it was sufficiently similar to be mistaken for his, it probably was a Volvo estate, possibly coloured green.'

'Where does that take us?'

'Not very far until we distinguish it from all the others belonging to the country brigade.'

'Then the case is on ice until we have the PM report – and likely that'll add nothing, so it'll stay frozen.'

'Yet remembering the bruises on the chest, the abrasions on the knuckles, the torn collar . . .'

'You presume I am forgetting all the facts?'

'No, sir.'

'That's something . . . Tyneside keeps asking for a witness statement from someone in south Athestone – here's the paperwork.'

Metcalfe reached across the desk to pick up the indicated file.

As he drove towards Inglewood, through the patchwork countryside which provided so rich a variety of terrain, Wyatt wondered whether it needed a physician, a neurologist, or a psychologist to explain why fear could so heighten a desire for sex. When the detective had asked Serena if she had noticed anything unusual about his appearance that Tuesday night, every nanosecond had been an hour of fear. Yet only minutes later, when walking around the garden with Leo, it had been wildly erotic thoughts of Estelle which had filled his mind, not a sense of wonderment at his escape.

He parked in sight of a restored twelfth-century priory. Tradition said the prior had been murdered by soldiers at the time of the dissolution of the monasteries; historians had proved no prior had been killed there at that time, but tradition was still preferred to truth. He switched on his mobile and dialled.

'Yes?' said Mabel.

'It's Tantalus.'

'She ain't free.'

'When will she be?'

'Can't say.'

'Will you tell her . . .'

The line went dead.

He often wondered if Mabel – middle-aged, built like a female all-in wrestler, wall-eyed, aggressive – was instructed to be as curtly unhelpful as possible because uncertainty and delay could be strong aphrodisiacs.

He drove on for three miles, parked in a natural lay-by, phoned again. Mabel was as curtly uncommunicative as before. He briefly considered turning back, accepting that, as did any specialist, Estelle worked to appointments; the thought of a fruitless conclusion was not one he could face.

The road crested a slight hill and Inglewood came into sight. Still an active market town, it had more charm in one street than Setonhurst could muster in all its hundreds. There were black-and-white-fronted family owned shops, Regency and Queen Anne town houses, a church with two walls which dated back to Saxon times, a genuine quintain – of course, all the parts had had to be renewed at different times – and the statue to Colonel Dillain, who had sent the 26th Lancers to a glorious death when drunkenly ordering a charge along the wrong valley. He parked in front of Colonel Dillain, phoned for the third time. When Mabel answered, he hurriedly said that if she'd just have a word with Estelle, he'd be very grateful . . .

'Don't promise nothing,' Mabel said before she replaced the receiver.

He drove along the bypass, which had been proposed many years before, been accepted and dismissed by various governments and governmental bodies, and had been built just before, rather than after as was the custom, the ever-increasing volume of heavy lorries finally choked Inglewood to a standstill; at the southern end, he turned off it into the town and in front of the public library, phoned for the fourth time.

'She'll see you if you get here fast,' Mabel said.

Excitement increased as he completed his journey; and with that excitement came self-contempt. In the lift in the newly built block of luxury flats expectation dried his mouth, tensed his stomach, raced his heart, as if he were a fourteen-year-old, about to enjoy his first experience of the female mysteries, yet he could not forget he was married, had sworn to forsake all others and keep only

Serena unto himself, was racing to break that oath. He prided himself on observing the old-fashioned standards which marked a gentleman, yet was eager to pay for what should – according to those standards (unless one was of an aristocratic lineage) – only be granted freely in married love, making his pretensions a mockery. He believed himself to be an intelligent man, yet would believe Estelle when she pressed her body against his and murmured words of love even while certain she had spoken the same words to another man only a short time before . . .

Conscience didn't just make cowards, it also succoured hypocrites.

It had taken over an hour to track down Hazel Seward in Athestone and a further exhausting forty minutes to persuade her that giving evidence concerning a road accident which she had witnessed would not result in the guilty driver's seeking her out and killing her. On his return to divisional HQ, Metcalfe expected to be bad-temperedly reminded by the DI that time was a detective's most precious commodity and that to waste it was . . . He had forgotten what day it was. On Saturdays, Horner's routine was to return home for lunch, leaving instructions that if anyone above the rank of superintendent wanted to speak to him, that person was to be told he was out on a priority call and as soon as he could be contacted would be in touch; superintendents and below must phone back later in the afternoon. Metcalfe placed the newly typed report on the desk in Horner's office and left.

In the CID general room, Carter was having an angry conversation over the phone. Metcalfe settled on the corner of the desk and waited.

Carter replaced the receiver. 'Bloody people! I ordered

a dozen Saturnia and the wife's just phoned to say the firm's sent Serenade.'

'Animal, vegetable, or mineral?'

'Can you be that ignorant?'

'If I try hard enough.'

'They're hybrid tea roses.'

'So now I'm a little less ignorant than I was . . . Is anything stirring here?'

'Nothing that's making waves. A couple of snatched handbags in the high street, shoplifting in the new supermarket in Elton Road, a mugging somewhere, I can't remember where, a crash which the Traffic boys are handling, and another moan from Old Annie, who swears that a man is stalking her again.'

'It must be full-moon time . . . If things are quiet, how about finding some grub?'

'The canteen's shut because the civilian staff have decided they won't work on Saturdays. It's only stupid sods like us who'll do that.'

'We can go to the pub round the corner.'

'The last time I ate there, I had rumble-guts all next day.'

'You should have added more water.'

'I had two halves of bitter, finish. The meat in the cottage pie was off.'

'We could try Chinese.'

'You don't get me eating in one of those places again; not after finding a dead insect in a spring roll.'

'Flied lice is a delicacy.' The witticism was received with the contempt it deserved.

Metcalfe returned to the lift and pressed the call button to the right of the doors, unsurprised that Carter, seldom responsive to anything that didn't immediately concern him, had failed to understand he was suffering a sharp bout of depressed loneliness and would have welcomed company during the meal.

He settled behind the wheel of the Fiesta. Return home and put one of the ready-made meals in the microwave? What could be lonelier than that? Better to drive across town to the Golden Cock, which offered company, plain but good cooking, and the possibility he might see one of the four snouts he ran.

Some forty minutes later, he was finishing a plateful of apple pie and ice cream when through the opened doorway of the dining room he saw Carpenter standing at the bar, round face sweating, tongue busy; from the laughter of those around him, his conversation was as ribald as ever. Metcalfe finished his meal, asked for and was given the bill, went through to the bar and handed this to the bartender together with a five-pound note; he pocketed the small change, made his way out to his car. No sign of recognition had passed between Carpenter and himself, yet the mark had been made and after a reasonable pause the other would come out and find him. He suffered the craving for a cigarette. When they'd married, he had smoked, Gwen hadn't; for months she had pleaded with him to give up because of the health risks and if anything happened to him, how could she cope on her own? He had stopped smoking. Then she, the non-smoker, had suffered the relatively early death. Many times since, he had been tempted to resume smoking – where now the necessary incentive to forgo the pleasure? – but had not succumbed; he couldn't explain why, unless it was the wish, never exactly expressed, not to let her down . . .

In the rear-view mirror, he watched Carpenter approach. The passenger door opened and Carpenter settled, over-flowing the front passenger seat; a man who smiled his way through life while his piggy eyes remained coldly calculating. 'Nice seeing you again, Mr Metcalfe.'

'How I'd like to believe you.'

'I've never told you a porky; never.'

'And I've just won the lottery rollover . . . I owe you one for that buzz on Scott, it was good.'

'Of course it was, Mr Metcalfe. Nothing but the best from me.'

Nothing that didn't carry a high price tag. Carpenter played the middle against the ends, the ends against each other. When he passed on information, it would be for reward, revenge, or clearing the decks for a future job he had lined up. 'Is there any word on the streets about Detective Sergeant Tobin?'

'Like what kind of word?'

'What kind d'you think? Someone had a fight with him before he died and I want to know who that was.'

'You think someone had it in for him?'

'I don't think they went to pat him on the head but missed. He's put people away who'd pay heavy to see him on the mortuary slab. I'm asking you to name the someone who did the paying.'

'There's been no talk.'

'Go on hearing nowt and you'll annoy me.'

'On me mother's grave, that's how it is.'

'You didn't have a mother.'

'If I've said so much as one word of a lie, may I be struck dead.'

'Get out of the car before it happens and there's a stinking mess to clear up.'

Carpenter giggled – a high-pitched, squeaky sound that seemed unlikely to have come from so large a frame. 'I swear there's silence. But if I ever hear a whisper . . .'

'You'll be on the blower before that whisper's died away.'

'You're unusual sharp, but then you would be, wouldn't you, him being one of yours?'

Carpenter's manner caused Metcalfe to say: 'Something amusing you? You think it's funny when one of us gets it?'

'That hurts. It really pains that you could think I would be laughing . . . I wish you didn't misunderstand me, Mr Metcalfe.'

'I understand you'd try to talk your way through the pearly gates.' Metcalfe was annoyed he could not judge why the other seemed unable to hide his amusement. It was out of character for him to show an emotion he must know would cause bitter anger . . .

'Would you be interested in who's become active in the high street?'

'Snatching handbags?'

'In one.'

'Give me some names.'

'Can't do that because they're foreign, from somewhere in Eastern Europe. A real smart team with a number three who's out of sight before a poor old dear can shout she's been fleeced.'

'Where do we meet up with them?'

'They're working from the Tavern Motel.'

'You know a lot – tried to buy their takings and been pushed?'

'As if I'd waste my time on pennies!' Carpenter laughed heartily and was still smiling as he climbed out of the car, puffing from the exertion.

Metcalfe watched him walk away towards a Jaguar. It was one more irony of life that law and order could often be maintained only with the help of those who defied both;

it was one more frustration that he was certain he had been fed the whereabouts of the street thieves to try to take his mind off the unusual slip Carpenter had made when he had allowed his amusement to become obvious.

Horner called Metcalfe into his office on Monday morning. 'They've pulled out their fingers and the final PM report's through.'

'What's it say, sir?'

Horner picked up a sheet of paper and briefly looked at it to refresh or check his memory. 'The skull was fractured and death was due to internal bleeding, the fracture is fully consistent with the head falling on the edge of a table. The bruises on the chest were not well defined because of the clothing and the fact that the force involved was not great. The bruises could have been inflicted by a fist, but there's nothing to prove they were . . . The forensics spend more time covering their own backs than doing their job . . . The abrasions on the knuckles of the right hand are consistent with the delivery of blows, but could follow contact with an inanimate object . . . More cover . . . No evidence was found of the pattern in the flesh reported by the doctor who made the initial examination of the body.

'Blood alcohol level was two hundred and fifty, which says he was tight tight.' Horner leaned back in his chair. 'So there's nothing to deny the possibility he was so pissed he smacked his hand into something, bruised his chest through hitting something, tripped over his own feet, fell and cracked his head on the table.'

'Equally, there doesn't seem to be anything to deny he did have a fight with someone. And unless he did have a fight, where did the collar come from?'

'A worn-out shirt, torn up for rags.'

123

'If Tobin was drunk, why's he going to go to a cupboard for a rag?'

'He was so tight it's illogical to expect him to act logically.'

'It's much more likely the collar was torn off the shirt of his assailant.'

'You need to remember the copper's prayer. Let the facts fit the theory, not the theory, the facts.'

Metcalfe silently wondered what else the other had just been doing.

Horner said: 'With the medical evidence ambiguous, we have to look very closely at other circumstances. If we assume there was an assailant, who would he have been? A casual intruder; an equally drunk friend who had an argument which ended in a fist fight; someone he'd put away in the past and was after revenge?' He sat upright. 'I'd expect anyone he'd nicked out for revenge after doing his bird would, drunk or sober, have used real force. And for what it's worth, your report . . .' Horner tapped a single sheet of paper on his desk, '. . . says none of your snouts has coughed up anything useful.'

'That's right. Only there was something . . .' Metcalfe became silent.

'Well?'

'Talking to one of 'em, I gained the impression there was something about the case which amused him.'

'What precisely?'

'I don't know.'

'Once again, you prefer impression to fact?'

'All I'm saying is, maybe he knows something which could explain the assault and for some reason he finds that funny.'

'Why didn't you squeeze it out of him?'

'He swore I was imagining.'

'Like as not, he was right . . . Was there a casual intruder? All doors and windows were secured and there was no sign of forced entry so no casual intruder. Was there a friend with whom he had a drunken row that ended in his death and the friend fleeing? The closed windows and locked and bolted doors say no friend. So it was accidental death . . .'

'That's not quite accurate,' Metcalfe said.

'What isn't?' Horner demanded with sharp annoyance.

'The front door wasn't locked and although one bolt was fully secured, the other was only halfway home.'

'You think he shut the door after his assailant had fled and he was laid out with a fractured skull?'

'It's possible.'

'A DC might possibly talk sense, but it never bloody happens.'

'Sir, part of the medical evidence was that a blow to the head which causes internal bleeding can result in what's called a latent period. The victim appears to be in control of himself, but then does something which involves stress and he suddenly dies. If he'd been bending over and having to use force to push home the bottom bolt, that could have been the stress.'

'If, might, perhaps . . . How often do I have to repeat that we work to facts, not imagination?'

'Aren't you forgetting the car parked outside the house?'

'I am not in the habit of forgetting evidence,' Horner snapped. 'And as to that, cars frequently park in front of other people's homes.'

'There's no suggestion that that would have been necessary because of the press of cars. It's a quiet road at all times.'

'Are you being argumentative for the pleasure of arguing?'

'No, sir. But I think that that car is important.'

'It could only be so if whoever had been driving it was in the house with Tobin.'

'And being parked there at that time surely suggests he was. I'm certain we need to identify whose car it was.'

'And how do you intend doing that?'

'The neighbour said it closely resembled Mr Wyatt's, which was often outside number twelve.'

'It wasn't his because he was with his sister all evening.'

'It means it was very likely a large Volvo estate, possibly green.'

'Have you learned anything more about it?'

'Unfortunately not.'

'Then I presume you're not suggesting we should try to identify this car with no other evidence to help us?'

'If we make a list of his friends and the names of villains he's put away who have recently come out, we can check what cars they run . . .'

'You tried to accuse me of forgetting evidence. You're forgetting that all the evidence points to him being on his own, so drunk he fell about, lightly injuring his hand and chest, before he crashed down onto the table, cracking his skull . . .'

'The evidence just isn't that conclusive.'

'I prefer probabilities, even if they can't be turned into certainties, to imaginative improbabilities . . .'

'Does that mean you're definitely putting the case in the dead file?'

'It does.'

'It doesn't matter it was one of us maybe murdered?'

'I accept facts and don't allow myself to be swayed by personal feelings.'

'I'd say that's exactly what you're doing by giving up.'

Horner's voice rose. 'My job is to make certain CID is run efficiently and within budget. Pursuing a very vague possibility which must entail hours of extra work and the considerable consequential additional expense, with the probability of attaining absolutely nothing, is neither efficient nor economically viable.'

'It's the extra effort which really worries you, isn't it?'

'That is insulting.'

'The truth often is,' Metcalfe said recklessly.

'Get out.'

He left.

Thirteen

It was policy in the county force that the divisional superintendent had administrative command of divisional CID. As a consequence, Metcalfe was called into the superintendent's office rather than the detective superintendent's office at county HQ.

Russell was a large man, both in character and build. He wore his seniority lightly and had a pragmatic approach to discipline, seeing it as a means of ensuring efficient continuity and not a measure of position. His attitude towards crime and criminals owed little to modern liberalism and his belief in the necessity of pure justice was unshakable. On his desk were small framed photographs of his wife and two sons, neither of whom had followed him into the police force because of his active dissuasion; for him, politics had long since held too much influence in policing and where politicians trod, there grew opportunism and corruption.

There was a knock on the door of his large office on the second floor. 'Come in.'

Metcalfe entered.

'Sit down.' A chair had been set in front of the desk; Metcalfe sat.

'I've called you in because of the formal complaint made against you. You know the nature of that complaint?'

'No, sir. I didn't know one was being filed.'

Russell's lips tightened, the only indication of his sharp annoyance. In his book, it was an inexcusable mistake not to have personally informed Metcalfe. 'Mr Horner says that you insulted him. He claims you explicitly and implicitly implied he was unconcerned about the death of Detective Sergeant Tobin and as a consequence was carrying out the investigation incompetently. Do you admit the charge?'

'No, sir.'

'You deny making any allegation?'

'Sir, I . . .'

'Well?'

'We had a difference of opinion about the future conduct of the case.'

'When Mr Horner said that he had decided the known facts did not warrant the further investigation you pro- posed, did you suggest this was because he was unwilling to face the extra work that would be involved?'

'Yes, sir.'

'A stupid allegation.'

Not if having worked for the DI for several years, one understood his character. 'I'm convinced the case isn't as straightforward as Mr Horner claims it to be.'

'You chose an extremely ill-conceived manner to express your opinion.'

'I may have spoken out of turn, but . . .'

'Would you like to explain why you made so stupid an accusation?'

'Because . . .'

'Well?'

'We ought to be looking everywhere for the truth, not closing the case down so that the person responsible gets away with it.'

'Something that, unfortunately, frequently happens.'

'When we can't go any further, when the evidence isn't strong enough or the rules prevent us presenting the evidence in court, not when we decide to close down before we've checked out every lead. There was someone in that house with Frank. I'm certain of that.'

'A certainty increased every time your opinion is challenged?'

'Because the facts spell it out.'

'Why are you so determined this case should be pursued in defiance of the detective inspector's decision?'

'Because . . . It'll probably sound ridiculous.'

'You will leave me to determine that.'

'I've always seen justice as the dividing line between civilization and chaos; every time a criminal gets away with his crime, that line is dented. It can only take so many dents before it breaks.'

'I like to think every officer in this division holds that opinion as firmly, but it is to be hoped that if expressed, it is not done in so robust a manner as you chose. I will have a word with Mr Horner and he may agree that since it can be said you were motivated by an excessive sense of dedication, not malice or the wish to be insolent, an apology would be a satisfactory conclusion. However, it will be within his right to insist on his complaint remaining on the book, in which case I will have no option but to convene a divisional disciplinary hearing.

'By the way,' Russell added casually, 'a dedication to the pursuit of justice is always well received by a disciplinary hearing, provided, that is, it is expressed in restrained, even modest terms.'

At four-thirty that afternoon, Metcalfe was called back to the superintendent's office.

'I have spoken to Mr Horner,' Russell said, 'and in view of your attitude, he cannot accept that it was a sense of excessive dedication to the job rather than insolence which prompted your words and he does not wish to withdraw his complaint. A disciplinary hearing will be convened as soon as possible.'

Small-minded, vindictive bastard, Metcalfe thought as he left the room and walked along to the lift. If the hearing found against him, he would earn a black mark and although there would be no practical consequences of this beyond a fine – only a hearing at county HQ before a civilian legal chairman could vary his pension rights – it would hurt his pride to leave the force under a slight cloud.

He had never liked shopping and when Gwen had been alive, had usually avoided doing any; since her death, he had been forced to learn the art of entering a supermarket, finding what he wanted, choosing between different brands, and resisting the purchase of items not on his shopping list.

He had just put two tins of baked beans in the shopping trolley – he still enjoyed them despite their being almost a staple diet because of the ease of preparation – when a woman said: 'Good evening, Alec.'

He turned to face Charlotte.

'Or should I say, Detective Constable Metcalfe?'

'Whichever you prefer,' he answered bad-temperedly, his mood still resentful.

She ignored his manner. 'Then I'll stick with Alec. I'm glad I've run into you . . .'

She had to stop as a woman pushed a trolley between them, forcing her to step back. After the other had passed, she said: 'They need a supermarket Rule of the Road.'

He finally responded to her friendliness. 'Traffic wardens would have a frustrating time.'

She smiled, was about to speak again when a couple passed between them. 'This is worse than Piccadilly Circus. Do you like coffee?'

'Yes.'

'Then how about some after we've finished shopping? Or would you prefer not to put up with a chattering female?'

'I can't think of a more pleasurable prospect.'

'Full marks for tact, but few for probable veracity . . . Have you much left to buy?'

'Very little.'

'Then let's say a quarter of an hour's time in the cafe next door.'

They separated and he finished his purchases at the delicatessen counter, where he bought two Scotch eggs which he hoped would for once be as tasty as they should be. As expected, insufficient checkout points were manned and he was forced to queue for several minutes before paying. He left the supermarket and walked the short distance to the cafe. Charlotte sat at a window table and he edged his way there, put the two plastic shopping bags down on the second chair opposite her. 'What can I get you?'

'I'm not up to coping with all the different kinds of coffee they're serving these days, so if you can find a simple white coffee, that's what I'd like . . . And we're going Dutch.'

'We're going English. I remember the doughnuts here are good. Will you have one?'

'I shouldn't.'

'That will make it taste twice as sweet.'

'Only if I can forget the bathroom scales . . . Has

132

anyone ever told you that you have a touch of the chameleon?'

'If I knew precisely what that really meant, I might answer you.'

She smiled.

He bought two doughnuts, two cups of coffee, carried the tray to the table, sat, passed one plate and one cup and saucer across.

She ate a mouthful. 'You're right – this is good.' She opened an individual pack of sugar and poured the contents into her cup. 'It reminds me of the village bakery when I was young. If I was there at the right time, they used to let me have a little of the doughnut mixture before they fried it; I thought it the most delicious taste in the world – I suppose now I'd find it pretty awful. And their cottage loaves had the most wonderful crusts, which I coated with farm butter . . . Rose-tinted memories! When you were young, did you live in town or country?'

'In north Setonhurst. I'm a local yokel.'

'More local than yokel . . . You prefer town to country?'

'Far from it, but the way things have worked out, I've not had the option. Maybe I'll move out into the country after I retire.'

'Which is when?'

'Very soon, thank goodness.'

'You're fed up with the job?'

'Not with the job, but with the conditions under which it now has to be carried out.'

'Would you like to expand on that?'

'And bore you?'

'I doubt it.'

He drank some coffee. 'It probably sounds very pi, but when I joined, I thought I'd be doing something really worthwhile for the community.'

'Why should that sound self-righteous?'

'People's attitudes have changed so much they can't understand that sort of attitude. These days, only number one counts and authority is always in the wrong.'

'Not everyone thinks like that.'

'There aren't many left who don't. The druggy bludgeons an old woman over the head to nick her last few quid so he can buy himself some more smack and he doesn't give a damn how injured she is, but if we catch up with him and he tries to fight us off and gets a thick ear, a crooked brief in court labels us sadistic thugs. Riots start up and when we try to cool things they turn on us and throw rocks and petrol bombs, use iron bars, and if we have to use force to defend ourselves, there'll be cameras turning and in the next news we'll be made to look like storm troopers. Then, instead of defending us, the politicians who demand we keep the peace at whatever cost to ourselves, not them, will rush to criticize us for using excessive force.'

'Were you thinking about all that when we met just now?'

'Why d'you ask?'

'You were hardly in a good humour.'

'That was because I'd just learned I was heading for a black entry.'

'I'm none the wiser.'

'An adverse entry in my flimsy.'

'You think that makes everything clear?'

'I'm going to be disciplined and that'll be noted in my service file.'

'Disciplined for what?'

'According to my superior, I was rude to him.'

'You called him a few names that used not to be in the dictionaries?'

'I told him . . .' He stopped.

'It cannot be repeated to delicate ears?'

'You almost had me rabbiting on about internal matters which aren't for publication.'

'My female curiosity is to be denied?'

'It is.'

'How annoying honourable behaviour can be.' She ate the last section of doughnut, drew a paper serviette out of the holder and wiped the sugar from her fingers. 'I refuse to estimate how many calories that was . . . Alec, there's something I want to ask you. Are you yet certain what really happened to Frank?'

'It's being listed as accidental death.'

'After your asking so many questions, we all began to think his death must have been suspicious.'

'It's because all those questions have been answered that it is an accident. I suppose you knew he was a heavy drinker?'

'Yes, I did.'

'When he died, he was very drunk. So it's surmised he lurched about the house, as drunks do, cannoned into the furniture and cracked his head on the table; that type of blow can cause an injury which doesn't prove fatal for some little time, which is why his body was found in the hall.'

'I suppose . . . I suppose it's a relief to hear that's what happened and no one else was involved. Which is being very selfish. Victoria's loss is the same, whatever . . . Thank you for telling me.'

'It'll be common knowledge very soon, so I've not betrayed any confidences.'

'Would anything short of the rack make you do that?'

He remembered her words with pleasure as he drove home.

*　　*　　*

135

The phone on the desk in the library rang; Wyatt reached across and picked up the receiver.

'It's Charlotte. I've just been talking to Alec.'

'Alec who?'

'Do we have to go through that again? The detective. I met him by chance at the supermarket and inveigled him into the cafe to try to find out what was happening.'

'Did you succeed?'

'The police have decided Frank died in an accident, on his own and very drunk.'

'You're saying the case is closed?'

'It is. You're in the clear and Serena will never have to know what happened unless Vicky chooses to speak out one day.'

'That'll never happen. She's forgetting all the sordid facts and building up a memory of Frank which will have him wearing a halo.'

'Why not, if that gives her relief.'

'It's so false.'

'Memories are always false.'

'It is quite certain the case is closed?'

'That's what Alec said.'

'Thank God the nightmare's over.'

After a few minutes, the conversation ended. He stared through the widow. Daylight was almost gone and a mist was forming; the nearby trees were not yet in leaf and their bare branches, smudged by the mist, formed an impressionistic tracery. Since he had learned of Frank's death – a week which seemed a year – he had lived in fear. Now that fear was over. He wondered why he felt exhausted rather than elated.

He needed a strong drink. He put the papers on which he'd been working – he'd always kept meticulous accounts – into a folder, left the library and went through to the sitting room, where Serena was watching television. She looked round as he entered. 'Who was that on the phone? I was going to answer, but you were first.'

'Charlotte rang me.'

Made uneasy by his tone of voice, she used the remote control to cut off the sound on the television. 'Is something wrong?'

'Nothing. She wanted to tell me she'd met the detective who's been here a couple of times and he told her that the police have decided Frank's death was an accident.'

'It's taken them long enough to decide that. Goodness only knows why they went on and on asking questions.'

'They had to make certain . . . Where's Vicky?'

'Leo was being very fractious so she's taken him up to bed and is reading to him in the hopes he falls asleep.'

'There's a very optimistic hope! Has she decided when she'll leave to stay with her friend?'

'She's not said anything to me. I hope she does soon because the change will do her so much good – with all the kids creating chaos, there won't be much time left for her to remember.'

'As the case is closed, presumably Frank's body will soon be released. Has she said if she still wants cremation and only the immediate family present?'

'She confirmed that a couple of days ago. Enid has promised to look after Leo whenever it is . . . I'm hoping that after everything's over, life will cheer up again for her.'

'You're thinking of Roger?'

'In time, him or someone else. Things have changed so much that it's become normal for a widow or widower to marry again . . . If I died tomorrow, I'd expect you to marry again.'

'If you were dead, how could you expect me to do anything?'

'You know what I mean,' she said, suddenly annoyed. 'Why do you so often make fun of what I say?'

'Because it prevents my becoming emotional.'

'Nothing will do that, although you hate to admit it . . . If I do die, my love, and you marry someone else, I hope she makes you as happy as you've made me. And as proud.'

Now she was attacking his conscience with a pickaxe.

Fourteen

The disciplinary hearing was held in the conference room before three senior officers from other divisions; Chief Superintendent Murrell, a pompous-looking man who was far from pompous in character, was chairman.

'You were not content to accept your senior officer's decision?' Murrell asked.

'I thought it was open to question, sir.' Metcalfe stood in front of the long table at which his judges sat. Behind him, a PC watched over the tape recorder and Russell and Horner were seated on an uncomfortable bench.

'You believed yourself more competent to judge than he?'

'I thought that while there was the slightest chance of uncovering the truth, that chance should be pursued.'

'Are you concerned in any way with setting the department's financial budget?'

'No, sir.'

'You could not, therefore, judge and balance out the various pressures that Mr Horner had to consider before reaching a decision?'

'Not from that point of view, no.'

'One might well say, you were arguing from ignorance.'

Metcalfe was silent.

'In circumstances of severe financial and manpower restraints, and where political considerations have to be observed however debilitating, command requires a balancing of all the pressures before a decision is reached. Ignorance precludes any right of criticism even when rank does not; in this instance, both considerations should have been observed.'

'I thought . . . I thought it had to be worthwhile trying to trace the car even if there was no certainty, only a possibility, of make and model. If we'd questioned all the friends and relations . . .'

'Mr Horner's decision was that the expense and man-hours which would have been involved were unlikely to be justified by the results achieved.'

'It was one way of making certain if anyone else was in the house; and if someone was, of identifying him.'

'In Mr Horner's opinion, the evidence suggests it is unlikely anyone was.'

'The evidence is open to a very different inter-pretation . . .'

'We are not here to judge the evidence.'

'But if—'

'You admit speaking the alleged words to your senior officer, so now all that is left before we retire to consider our verdict is to ask if you have anything further to say.'

'Sir, I've apologized before for what I said and I do so again, unreservedly. But I was so convinced we had to pursue every possible lead, however unlikely to produce results, because otherwise we were not going to get anywhere. And if someone else was present in the house, there had to be the possibility the case was one of manslaughter or murder. Every time a person commits a crime and gets away with it, justice gets kicked and chaos comes a little closer . . .'

140

'You may presume that we are fully aware of the importance of law and order to a democracy; and of the consequences of crime and disorder.'

'Yes, sir.'

'We note that you claim the words addressed to Mr Horner were the product of over-zealousness rather than insolence. This will not, of course, excuse a breach of the rules of conduct. A senior officer is to be treated by his juniors with respect at all times, not because of any presumed personal superiority, but because of his superior rank.

'We will now retire.'

Twenty minutes later, Murrell, flanked on either side by his fellow judges, was once more seated at the table. He removed his glasses, wiped them with a handkerchief, replaced them. The PC in charge of the tape recorder suddenly fiddled with the controls, his expression uneasy; then he relaxed as the machine once more functioned correctly.

Murrell said: 'Detective Constable Metcalfe, you have been charged with disrespectful conduct towards a senior officer. Since you agreed you spoke the alleged words to Mr Horner, we do not have to decide whether, indeed, they were addressed to him. We are left, therefore, to decide the nature of your culpability. In our judgement, you were motivated by excessive zeal and not malice.

'You are fined one hundred pounds and an entry will be made to this effect in your records.'

There was a brief pause before Murrell continued speaking. 'We should like to make it clear that we find it unfortunate this matter could not have been dealt with informally.'

Metcalfe stood as they left the room. No winner, no real loser. He hoped that made Horner feel sour.

Horner had refused the invitation to Metcalfe's evening retirement party, held in the private room of the Red Lion; no one was surprised. Russell had a couple of small whiskies and then left, pleading the pressure of work; senior officers felt bound to remain sober – when observed by juniors – and he realized this was liable to make him a drag on proceedings.

As the evening proceeded, Reg Carter began to recite 'Albert and the Lion' and this melded into an obscene version of 'The Boy Stood On the Burning Deck' and few noticed the substitution. Boyne challenged everyone to a hairy leg contest and took off his trousers to the jeers of the WPCs present and the cheers of a couple of tarts who claimed they had been invited to the party, but were unwilling to name by whom. Seal was very sick. The landlord tried to end proceedings at eleven and succeeded just before midnight by refusing to provide any more drink, no matter how much he was offered.

Taxis were ordered because if a policeman was found drunk in charge of a car his career was blown and his pension a memory. Boyne left with the two tarts and to much shouted advice.

Metcalfe was driven to Barkend Street. He paid the driver, added a large tip, made his uncertain way along the imitation York paving stone to the front door and had a frustrating time trying to insert the key in the lock. Once inside the house, he decided another little drink wouldn't do him any harm.

He poured out a large gin and a splash of tonic, weaved a way through to the front room, proudly placed the glass down on the table without spilling any of the liquid, collapsed on to the settee. He stared at the far wall, shut his eyes because it was disturbing to see it move with a waving motion. Retired. Finished, the camaraderie; beginning, endless, solitary time. Perhaps he'd find a job as a security guard to fill in some of that time. But Alf . . . Or was it Fred? . . . Maybe it was George . . . had said what a bloody awful job that was. He could now and then visit the boys at the station and chat with them, but time would soon alienate. He'd seen that happen. Retired policemen turning up and boring newcomers with their reminiscences . . .

He reached across for the glass, knocked it over and the gin and tonic splashed down onto the floor. Sodding typical of life.

Fifteen

At the beginning of the third week in May, the uncertain weather which had hitherto plagued the month gave way to warm, sunny days with light southerly winds. Bredgley Hall, flower beds filled with colour, majestic oaks in full leaf, lawns banded by mowing and almost as immaculate as bowling greens, provided a beauty that was timeless. Standing ten feet out from the portico and massive front door, Wyatt viewed the scene with a pride that was untouched by any hint of guilt of privilege. He had no time for modern hypocrisy. He had inherited and earned a great deal of money and could have spent much of it on ephemeral pleasures, but instead he had restored the property to its present state and saved a piece of English history.

Serena, a trug in her right hand, came round the eastern corner of the house. 'I wondered where you were . . . I've just had an exhausting time. I told John I wanted peas for lunch and he tried everything he could think of to refuse to pick any of those very early ones for me; said the pods weren't full and would need at least another fortnight. I tried for the umpteenth time to explain we liked our vegetables young, sweet and tender, but all he could do was look at some distant horizon with a vacant expression.'

'Dreaming of finding a job with someone who wants

to grow four-hundred-pound pumpkins which can be exhibited at a local show.'

'I doubt even he could grow anything that weight.'

'I think you'll find the record for a pumpkin in this country is more than that; and, of course, they'll grow even bigger in the States . . . I see you did finally manage to get him to pick what you wanted.' He reached into the trug and brought out a pod.

'No doubt resentfully.'

He split the pod between thumb and forefinger, rolled the small peas onto the palm of his hand, popped them into his mouth.

'Are they sweet?' she asked.

'As a virgin's kiss. But how far would one have to travel these days to verify that comparison?' The moment he'd spoken, he regretted the words as her expression showed they had disturbed her. 'What are we having with the peas?' he asked quickly.

'A leg of lamb. The butcher swore it would be more tender than the last one, which I complained about; he said that was Scottish, which was why it was tough.'

'A true Sassenach.'

'I must go in and check the weight and see if it's time to put it in the oven . . . By the way, Vicky phoned. She's decided not to sell Athin Road, but to have it redecorated. While that's being done, she'll probably stay here.'

'She reckons redecoration will be the answer to memories?'

'I suppose she does. I think she's wrong, but it has to be her decision . . . She was complaining that Leo is becoming impossible. As I said, of course he is, he's a boy. One other thing. She very casually mentioned that Roger had been in touch to ask her to have a meal some time. Wanted to know what I thought of the idea.'

'What did you reply?'

'That in her position, I'd say yes.'

'Would you?'

'Of course . . . Well, maybe not. But as we have to keep telling ourselves, times have changed so much and her generation doesn't see the world as we did. If she can find happiness again, why shouldn't she?'

'Logically, no reason at all.'

'He's such a pleasant boy.'

'I imagine he'd prefer to be called a man.'

'He's far nicer than Frank, though I shouldn't say that with Frank dead.'

'As someone pointed out, death only sanctifies those who need sanctifying.'

'I could never understand why she married . . . It's all water under the bridge.'

'Let's hope it's not tidal and returns.'

'What's that supposed to mean?'

'I've no idea.'

'Sometimes I find it hard to understand you.'

'The recipe for a perfect marriage.'

Metcalfe was bedding out some plants in the small back garden when he thought he heard the door bell. He stood, brushed dusty earth from hands and knees, went through the house to open the front door.

'I was just about to clear off, thinking you weren't here,' Carter said.

'I was out at the back, gardening.'

'Never reckoned that was one of your hobbies.'

'It isn't, but I decided I had to do something to cheer up the garden so I'm bedding some pansies.'

'Didn't reckon that was one of your hobbies, either.'

'Your humour hasn't improved . . . Come on in and have a jar.'

In the front room, Metcalfe asked: 'Gin, whisky, or lager?'

'Make it a lager, as I've got to report back to the Guv'nor.'

'You're on duty?'

'Been sent to have a word with you.'

'About what?'

'Talking's difficult with a dry throat.'

Metcalfe left and went along the short corridor to the kitchen and larder. He poured out two lagers, opened a bag of crisps and emptied these into a soup plate, returned to the front room.

'Things are bloody,' Carter said, as he took one tumbler.

'Why so?'

He helped himself to several crisps as Metcalfe sat. 'The new Guv'nor's moved in. You'd not heard?'

'Not a word. Is it George Acton as the fortune-tellers prophesied?'

'In person and hell-bent on promotion and driving us poor sods into the ground to get it for him.'

'So he's working you harder than Horner did?'

'That's comparing a Ferrari with a bicycle. First thing he said to us was there'd be no clock-watching in his team. Overtime often doesn't go down in the books because, according to him, the job's more important than the man.' He drank deeply. 'We're all on our knees.'

'In homage?'

'Exhaustion. And if he wasn't enough, there's your replacement.'

'What's wrong with him?'

147

'The only thing between his ears is wet cotton wool.'

'He'll shake down, given time.'

'Give him five years and he won't be any different . . . You're dead lucky to be out of it all!'

Carter envied him because he was out of it; he envied Carter for still being in it. When a man was content with life he was probably dead. 'So what's brought you here when you're suppose to be on duty – the need to recuperate?'

'I told you, the Guv'nor sent me.'

'I thought you were hallucinating. To do what?'

Carter drained his glass. 'That was very welcome.'

'You'll risk the other half?'

'Always like to be friendly.'

Carter, Metcalfe thought sardonically as he stood, was living up to his reputation – the possessor of an endless thirst when someone else was paying. But company was company. He held out his hand for the empty tumbler, left.

When he returned and handed over the filled glass, he said: 'You were about to tell me why the DI sent you here.' He sat.

'He's some work for you.'

'You didn't think to remind him I'm retired.'

'Of course I did, and got my head bitten off for my pains.'

'Then what gives?'

'I'm just the messenger.'

'You don't know what it's all about?'

'That's right.'

'Seems odd.'

'He's bloody odd. If they didn't break the mould after he was born, they goddamn well should have done.'

*　　*　　*

Acton had wiry black hair, a high forehead, a Roman nose, a firm mouth, and a very square chin; his dark brown eyes were sharp; his body was muscular, thanks to regular exercise, and his movements had the precision of someone who seldom wasted energy.

He shook hands with Metcalfe, his grip firm but not aggressive. 'Thanks for coming in. Hope it hasn't disturbed anything?'

'No problem, sir.' Rank always liked to be acknowledged, even when the recipient denied this or no longer had that right to demand it.

'Grab a seat.'

Metcalfe sat on the uncomfortable wooden chair in front of the desk. It didn't need Carter's description quickly to recognize the new DI to be a man whose ambition was to get to the top because he considered that to be his rightful position.

Acton opened a file on his desk, but studied Metcalfe rather than the papers in it. 'Shortly before your retirement, you appeared before an internal disciplinary hearing on an insubordination charge. In your defence, you expressed a very strong belief in justice and the need, almost right, to pursue your interpretation of what that was. It is because of that expressed belief and because you are retired and therefore able to act without arousing interest here that I decided to speak to you. You will treat everything I say to you in strictest confidence. Is that clear?'

'Yes, sir.' He had not been asked if he were willing to return to work. Acton was a man who assumed his will would be done.

'Strictest confidence means there will be no discussion with any other officer, of whatever rank, serving or retired. If asked what you are doing, as no doubt you will be, you

149

will provide an answer that satisfies curiosity, but gives no hint as to the truth.' Acton leaned back in his chair. 'I think I can trust you implicitly to observe those orders.'

If that were meant to be an accolade, Metcalfe thought, it was hardly an enthusiastic one.

'Yesterday afternoon, the detective chief superintendent phoned me from county HQ to tell me the DI of E Division has reported that one of their snouts claims there's been a member of CID in this division on the bung for years.'

'That's bloody ridiculous!'

'I hope so.'

'I know they're all dead straight.'

'A clever man makes certain his mates never suspect him.'

'Who's it supposed to be?'

'If I'd been told, I'd be approaching the problem from a different direction.'

'Then it's just rumour.'

'There can be fact inside a rumour.'

'But usually isn't.'

'You'll find out into which category this information falls. When you were active, you were running how many snouts?'

'Three, occasionally four.'

'Start by squeezing them. A bent copper is rare, thank God, but when one's around, the news spreads; villains like to think we're no better than them.'

'They'll know I've retired and can't do 'em any favours so they'll want their palms heavily greased before their tongues wag.'

'When you reckon the info could be solid, pay; you'll be refunded in full . . . How close were you to the other members of CID?'

'Mostly, it was a working relationship with not much more than the usual pub visits for relaxation. Apart from anything else, later on there was the difference in ages – like as not, they called me grandpa when I wasn't listening.'

'Were any of them enjoying an extravagant life?'

'Only the DS and he'd his wife to thank for that.'

'No hints of heavy betting, women, expensive meals, gold Rolex?'

'Nothing like that.'

'I don't have to tell you I'm hoping you can prove the story is complete balls.'

More like praying he succeeded in doing that, Metcalfe decided. In theory, because this accusation concerned divisional CID before Acton had taken command, he should not be tainted even if it was proved true; in practice, he almost certainly and unfairly would be and that might well affect his chances of high promotion.

'You haven't asked what your pay will be, I assume because you're happy to have the chance to clear the department's reputation . . . You'll be on an hourly rate which will be the equivalent of a constable of five years' service. And no overtime. I tried to squeeze a better offer out of Accounts, but they refused to be squeezed.'

'Will you want a diary kept with all hours logged?'

'Accounts will. They'd demand George Washington showed them the axe as well as the tree.'

'I reckon I'll need to start by talking to the snout who provided the info.'

'Whoever's running him will, as usual, be very loath to give a name; he'll probably refuse.'

'Then call on the DCS to apply pressure. Since he's so stupid as to think there could be any truth in the allegation, he must accept he has to give us every chance of proving he's wrong.'

'In the short time you've been retired, you seem to have forgotten that one does not call a detective chief superintendent stupid or dictate to him what he must do . . . I'll try to find the name by more conventional means.'

Sixteen

Metcalfe drove the twenty-one miles to Aston Cross and on the northern outskirts turned into the council car park on the opposite side of the road to the White Knight. He climbed out of the Fiesta and visually searched for a dark blue Ford Focus, saw it, threaded his way between the cars to reach it. The woman behind the wheel looked up at him. Experience enabled him to place her accurately – a tart approaching an age at which the quality of the customers would deteriorate quickly and perhaps dangerously.

As he came to a halt, she lowered the window. 'Deirdre?' he asked.

'Yeah.'

'Shall we go across and have a drink?' He indicated the square building from which, whenever the traffic eased off, came the sounds of many people.

'Not in there.'

Because there might be someone who instinctively identified him as a detective, which would place her in danger? 'I'm not at home in this town; where do you suggest?'

'The West Cliff Court.'

He knew the hotel by reputation. It seemed she was determined to profit all she could from this meeting. 'OK. My car's over there . . .'

'We'll go in mine.'

When he settled on the front passenger seat, he wondered if she suffered an instinctive fear of getting into a policeman's car.

She was a good, confident driver. The movement of her legs as she accelerated and braked caused the hem of her dress to ride up her thighs and she made no effort to pull it down. He was annoyed to find himself watching to see how high it would reach.

The West Cliff Court, on the London road, was large, architecturally ugly, which made the decision to floodlight it at night a strange one, and surrounded by extensive lawns and many flower beds. As was to be expected, after they had parked and walked towards the large and ostentatiously ornamental main entrance, the uniformed doorman made no move to open the wide glass doors for them – having identified the nature of Deirdre's calling, a further brief glance assured him Metcalfe was of no social, media, or celebrity standing.

The expansive foyer, an example of luxury taken to a tactless extreme, was aimed at delighting those whose money was fresh. The bar into which she led him was all chrome, leather, and gold stars. They sat in one of the topless alcoves and waited until a waiter could be bothered to come across.

'You want your usual?' the waiter asked her.

'Sure.'

He turned to Metcalfe. 'And you . . . sir?' The pause was not quite long enough to be openly insulting.

'I'll have a lager, please.'

'We don't serve beer or lager in this bar . . . sir.'

'Then a gin and tonic.'

'Gordon's, Booth's, Plymouth, Gilbey's, or Seager's . . . sir?'

Metcalfe allowed his irritation to surface. 'Burrough's Extra Dry.'

There was a pause. 'We don't have any at the moment,' the waiter said tightly.

'Then I'll have Gordon's.'

He left.

'You annoyed him,' Deirdre said, relaxing for the first time since they had met.

'I hope so,' Metcalfe answered. 'You obviously come here quite often?'

'Not as often as I used to.'

He wondered if she saw her future as clearly as he did or, like the majority of tarts, lived only for the day.

The waiter returned and put a coaster, with the hotel's name in gold and red, in front of each of them, glasses on the coasters, and small glass bowls of toasted almonds and stuffed olives between them.

She drank eagerly.

'What's that you're having?' he asked.

'Champagne cocktail.'

It was to be hoped Acton would view the bill without blinking. In such a place, a champagne cocktail would cost an arm and a leg – even if the glass held only fizzy lemonade and a lump of sugar so that she and the barman could later share the profit. 'You've been saying you know a bent split.'

'Not me.'

'Who, then?'

'A punter.'

'What's his name?'

'Give over.'

'Come on.'

'It wouldn't get you nowhere. His mouth's as tight as his purse.'

'But he talked to you.'

'Pillow talk. Only he has a queer idea of what a pillow's for.' She fiddled with the stem of her glass. 'I was a bloody fool to speak. But since I'm still alive, I mean to stay that way.'

'He's a hard villain?'

'A man and that's all you're getting.'

'I could work it so that you never came into the picture.'

'And perhaps you couldn't. He starts thinking I'm a mouth and I'm dead, or wishing I was. You think my phone will ring if I've more scars on my face than a dog has fleas?' She drained the glass.

'It could be worth heavy money.'

'The dead don't spend. Haven't you been listening? No name.'

'I need one or I'm anchored.'

'Your problem.'

Their waiter came up to their alcove. 'Mademoiselle would like another drink?' he said, making a statement. He picked up her glass, then said, his gaze fixed inches above Metcalfe's head: 'The tropical bar has Burrough's Extra Dry. I will get some . . . sir.' He picked up Metcalfe's glass.

'Don't bother with that – I just wondered if you served it. I'll have another Gordon's.'

As the waiter walked away, she said, 'He's thinking of sticking a knife in your back.'

'Then he's no expert. Knives in the back stick in bone; it's knives in the belly that go deep.'

The waiter returned, placed glasses in front of them, left.

She picked up an olive and ate. 'Are you going to drink that?'

'Why not?'

'He's likely spat in it.'

'A creep like him hasn't the guts to do more than see there's not a full measure of gin. Waste not, want not.'

'If only things were that easy.'

'And if they were?'

She drank, put the glass down on the coaster, fiddled with the stem. 'Like always, it's what I haven't got I want most.'

'Such as?'

'A different life . . . Shit! There's me talking things I keep under the tongue even after the sixth drink.' She looked at her wristwatch. 'I need to get back soon.'

He left the waiter a tip designed to confirm the other's judgement that he was a lumpen prole.

Twenty minutes later, she drove into the council car park and braked to a halt near his car. He put his hand on the door handle, but did not immediately activate it. 'If I guarantee . . .'

'A machine always bloody fails the day after the guarantee comes to an end.'

He opened the door and climbed out.

'I'd tell you if . . .'

He bent down until his head was level with hers. 'If what?'

'It wouldn't cost me too hard. Know why? Because you never angled for a freebie – there ain't many like that.'

He waited, expecting her to continue speaking, but she stared through the windscreen, her expression bitter. He shut the door and she drove off.

Seventeen

M etcalfe walked past the open doorway of the CID general room, came to a halt when there was a shout of, 'Alec.'

He turned back and stepped inside.

'I thought it was your ugly mug,' Jamieson said. 'What's dragged you back?'

'To have a word with the Guv'nor. There's some sort of query regarding a past case and he asked me to drop in and talk it over when I could.'

'You were favoured to be given such latitude.'

'He's strong medicine? Bit of a change from Horner, then. Must cause a load of grief, having to work hard for a living.'

'I'm not saying that.'

Metcalfe was amused Jamieson should be reluctant to admit to any criticism of Horner's command – adverse comments concerning one's own department, past or present, were kept within the department; his retirement might not have made him a complete outsider, but it had happened long enough ago to make certain he was not still an insider.

For ten minutes, he and Jamieson chatted, then he left and walked past the detective sergeant's room – when asked how the newcomer, Crowe, was shaping up, Jamieson's reply had been a noncommittal 'Could be worse' – and along to the detective inspector's room. He knocked on the partially opened door, went in.

'Shut the door,' Acton said.

He shut the door, turned and faced the desk. 'I saw Deirdre last night, sir. I did my damnedest, but she refused to give the name either of the mouth who gave her the info or of the split concerned.'

'You offered a generous pay-off?'

'It didn't have any attraction. She obviously entertains a variety of punters and this one is a hard villain. If he gets to thinking she's been grassing, she'll end up badly scarred or in an oblong box.'

'I imagine you told her things could be worked so no one could ever judge who'd talked?'

'She wasn't buying the possibility.'

'A pity . . . All right, you need to get out on the streets and keep your ears sensitive. Have you checked what help your snouts can give?'

'There's not been time to do that yet.'

Instead of suggesting time was made by those with the initiative to make it, as Horner would have done, Acton said: 'Get on to that as soon as you can.'

Metcalfe hesitated, then said: 'Last night created a bit of a problem.'

'Which is?'

'When I met Deirdre, I suggested a chat in a pub: she insisted on the West Cliff Court.'

'That surprised you?'

'The cost of the drinks did.'

'Not one of your watering places? No call for panic. Give me the receipt and you'll be repaid at the bureaucrats' leisure.'

'I haven't got it with me.'

'When you bring it in, it's to come into my hands and not be left on the desk. Clear?'

'Yes, sir.'

'What was she drinking to get you so worried?'

'Champagne cocktails.'

'An awful waste of champagne.'

The lack of information, even the hint of any, over the past thirty-six hours meant that by Wednesday evening, Metcalfe's mood was pessimistic. He walked into the Golden Cock and ordered a drink, stared bleakly at the ancient mirror behind the bar, which was engraved with an advertisement for Gordon's gin. Acton was not a man to react kindly to failure.

'What's it to be, mate?' one of the bartenders asked.

He ordered a gin and tonic. Gordon's, not Burrough's Extra Dry . . . He wondered if Deirdre was entertaining; did the image of a dread future creep ever closer . . . His thoughts jumped as in the mirror fronting him, he saw the overweight, smiling Carpenter whose piggy eyes sometimes revealed more of his character than he would have wished. His reflection moved from right to left, disappeared. The bartender brought Metcalfe his drink and he paid. From his left came loud laughter. Carpenter entertaining his listeners with one of his obscene jokes?

He had a second drink, then went out to his car and settled behind the wheel. He wondered why he imagined it possible that Carpenter would provide any useful information when his other snouts had been as useful as a broken corkscrew. . . Yet again, he had to accept memory was a mystery. Why should he suddenly remember his previous visit to the Golden Cock and his anger when Carpenter had appeared to be amused by the questions, which had implicitly suggested that one

160

of the possible motives for Tobin's death that was being considered was that someone he'd helped put away in the past had exacted revenge . . . ?

Carpenter opened the front passenger door and, to the accompaniment of much puffing, settled on the seat. 'Didn't expect to see you again, Mr Metcalfe.'

'Unexpected pleasures are always better.'

'When I see you standing at the bar, I first wondered if you was wanting a word, but then I remembered you was retired. So I reckoned you were just enjoying yourself and I said to myself, why not say hullo to an old friend?'

'I'm touched you should welcome a chat for old time's sake and not because your conscience's so grubby you get a bellyache from worry every time you see the law, even if it's retired.'

Carpenter chuckled.

'Do you remember the last time we had a chat?'

'Can't say I do,' he replied carefully.

'Frank Tobin had been found dead at home.'

'Nasty accident. A young man like him needed many more years to enjoy himself.'

'Why are you so certain it was an accident?'

'Ain't been no movement.'

'Lack of evidence. And now we've mentioned the circumstances of our last chat, you'll remember I asked for the name of someone he'd helped put away who'd come out and was feeling aggrieved. Know your response?'

'Can't say I do.'

'You said we would be very keen, wouldn't we, since he was one of us.'

There was a silence which Carpenter finally broke. There was a note of unease in his voice when he said: 'Fair enough, Mr Metcalfe. Being coppers, you would all be real keen.'

'But when you said that, you were laughing inside.'

'Never.'

'And when I asked why, you changed the conversation real sharp by giving me details of the team which was blagging on the High Street.'

'I don't remember none of that.'

'Try harder.'

'Why are you going on like this now you're out of it?'

'Residual curiosity.'

'Don't seem natural.'

'Even in heaven, there's an awkward squad. So why was it?'

'Straight, I don't know.'

'You're sure?'

'Couldn't be surer.'

'We picked up three out of four of the team that day. Came from the Balkans and were as rough a bunch as you could meet. The bench was soft and listened to their stories of poverty and persecution and only handed out oncers. But it got 'em off the streets for a while.'

'I did you a good turn, then?'

'But you did yourself a bad turn.'

'How d'you mean?'

'Like I said, we got three out of four. The missing joker is a brother to one of 'em inside and I'm told that where they come from, people think nothing of slicing off various parts of someone they don't like; it's just good, dirty fun.'

'You're not . . .'

'Not what?'

'Saying you'd let on who gave the word?'

'We're beginning to understand each other.'

'But you're retired!'

'Doesn't stop me having a leaky mouth.'

'Mr Metcalfe, you wouldn't do that.'

'I promise you, only if I have to.'

'But why?'

'I've explained.'

There was a second, and much longer, silence.

'What you really asking?' Carpenter finally muttered.

'Why were you laughing inside when I spoke about Frank Tobin's death?'

Carpenter spent time licking his thick lips. 'You mean, you still ain't suspected?'

'Suspected what?'

'He was on the make.'

'You'll have to do better than that if you don't want to lose your ears, nose, and pecker.'

'For Christ's sake, that's how it was, straight. There was you, as innocent as a young lag doing bird for the first time, telling me how the coppers wanted to learn who had it in for him, there was me knowing it was most likely someone he'd sold duff information, but you'd no idea he was in on that racket. But I wasn't laughing; on me mother's grave, I wasn't.'

Acton, speaking on the telephone, looked up as Metcalfe entered. He gestured with his free hand and Metcalfe lifted up one of the chairs set against the wall, positioned it in front of the desk, sat. The conversation was an ill-tempered one.

Acton replaced the receiver. 'Well?' he said, his tone sharp.

'I've spoken to the last of the snouts I used to run, sir.'

'With any result?'

'He gave me the name of an officer he claims was on the make.'

'Who?'

'Detective Sergeant Tobin. But I find that very difficult to believe.'

'You're accusing someone on evidence you don't believe?'

'Sir, I'm making no accusation, just repeating what I was told last night.'

Acton stood, turned, took three steps across to the window and looked out. After a moment, he said: 'I apologize. It was a report which needed to be made in the terms in which you made it. My immediate response was a knee-jerk, illogical reaction to something I didn't want to hear.' He returned to his seat. 'How sound is your informer?'

'I'd never risk my life on his word. He's a tricky bastard who plays everything tight to his chest. But what keeps worrying me is that I had to put the frighteners on him before he'd name.'

'So he was perhaps giving solid evidence, however unwelcome, for his own safety. And you're afraid your disbelief is an emotional response?'

'I suppose so. And yet . . . A copper goes crook for the bung, doesn't he?'

'Usually it is for thirty pieces of silver, yes.'

'Frank married into money and there obviously wasn't any need for extra.'

'There's always a desire for extra, if not a need. Is his wife wealthy in her own right?'

'I can't say, but I've always assumed she was.'

'Why?'

'They had a great lifestyle.'

Acton picked up a pencil and fiddled with it. 'It sometimes isn't money. It can be a warped sense of revenge leading to a desire to mock the law.'

'Doesn't sound like Frank.'

'If you never suspected him and yet he was crook, your judgement carries no weight.'

'I suppose not.'

'Was there any suggestion he bore a resentment against the force?'

'None I ever came across.'

'Were there signs of his being friendly with known villains?'

'Never heard of any.'

'Then we're back to money.'

'Which just doesn't make sense.'

'As you've said. What I'm saying is that perhaps circumstances aren't as you present them.'

The phone rang. Acton lifted the receiver and spoke, becoming curter with every sentence. He replaced the receiver, made a note, looked up and said: 'First thing to learn is whether he spent more than he earned.'

'There can't be any doubt on that score.'

'Then we're going to need proof of where the extra came from, which means speaking to the wife and learning if she was funding him. But it'll need to be done with every ounce of subtlety you can manage. If the family thinks we're accusing Tobin of having been an informer and we can't prove he was, they'll start shouting we're damning the dead and the shit will hit the fan. There's nothing the media likes better than to have the chance to criticize us. Funny how their attitude suddenly becomes all warm if one of them gets personally touched by crime.'

Eighteen

M etcalfe finished his lunch – a convenience beef meal and ice cream; the beef had had a closer than usual relationship to leather, the Yorkshire pudding would have been disowned by that county, the potatoes had been floury, the broccoli stemmy, but the ice cream had been tasty – and settled in one of the two armchairs in the front room. The siesta was rightly scorned as a Latin decadence by every right-minded Englishman and he began to read the newspaper. He awoke an hour and a quarter later and for a brief moment panicked, convinced he would arrive back at the station late for duty; then reality returned. In retirement, it had become difficult to be late for anything.

After a while, his mind returned to the problem of how to uncover evidence that would either absolve or convict Frank Tobin of being a traitor. Bribery always left a trail, but where did he start looking for that trail, remembering that the wealth of the Wyatt family might well explain what would otherwise be suspicious? Did he ask if they had given their daughter a large allowance and if so, had she passed some of that on to him? Surely that was inadvisable. Not only was it putting the cart before the horse, more specifically, it might well prove impossible to learn the answers without arousing the Wyatts' anger. No, first he had to uncover evidence that would warrant taking such a risk. If this existed, where did he start looking for it? . . . The previous year, Frank had taken the family to the West Indies for a holiday and had later made a point of telling everyone about its many luxuries. How much would that have cost? To find the answer would require knowing which firm he had booked through and only the family could quickly and easily answer that . . . He remembered the larder at Frank's house. In the metal racks under the shelving had been many bottles (and nearby an unopened case) of Laphroaig malt, fewer of Lanson Black Label champagne, Pommard burgundy, Cinzano, and Gordon's gin, plus a couple of cases of cans of lager. A 'cellar' one would not expect to find in a detective sergeant's home; possibly even the chief constable's was not so richly stocked. Was this an unusual quantity, or relatively normal? Bought with money that came from the Wyatts or from a different source? How to determine which? The average supermarket might well not stock such relatively expensive champagne, whisky, or burgundy; if one of them did, what chance was there of tracing buyers? More likely, the purchases had been made in an off-licence, a much more hopeful source of information . . .

Forty-five minutes later, he walked into the small off-licence in Thornby which had survived all competition because it was a wealthy town in which lived many who preferred service to self-service and were prepared to pay for quality.

The man behind the long mahogany counter on which were bottles of famous burgundies and Bordeaux (emptied by a previous owner many years before) was short, pointed, wore a toupee, and possessed of a manner that was deferential without descending into servility.

'Good afternoon, sir. How may I help you?'

'By giving me some information. DC Metcalfe, divisional CID,' Metcalfe answered, as he quickly produced his temporary warrant card, wishing to make it clear he was not about to order a dozen Krug Grande Cuvée.

'Dear me. Is there some trouble?'

'None, but it's possible you can help us.'

'Which I will naturally do if that's possible.'

'We're interested in identifying someone who's very fond of Laphroaig whisky and may have bought some here.'

'An expensive malt but, if I may say so, worth every penny. Or should I say, every pound?'

Metcalfe smiled a tactful appreciation of the little witticism. 'Would it be usual for someone to buy a dozen bottles at a time?'

'Not, unfortunately, as usual as it would once have been. Nevertheless, we certainly do have clients who present large orders and favour the best malts.'

'Would you be able to name anyone who's recently come in and ordered a dozen bottles?'

'Regular clients usually have a little chat so I do learn their names.'

'Then you can tell me who's been buying Laphroaig by the case?'

The owner hesitated. 'I'm not certain that would be in order.'

'How's that?'

'It would be breaching customer confidentiality.'

Metcalfe was amused, rather than annoyed, by the other's dated manner. He said reassuringly: 'No one will ever learn about their drinking habits.'

'I do assure you no criminal would ever come in here to buy his wine, or even spirits.'

These days, it was the successful criminal who could

168

afford to live luxuriously; the owner was not only from the past, he still lived there. 'The chap we're trying to identify likely hasn't helped himself to so much as a packet of crisps in the whole of his life.'

'Then I don't understand why you wish to know who he might be.'

Metcalfe thought an appeal to patriotism would probably help. 'State security; very hush-hush. If I say a single word more, I'll be sent to the Tower to have my head chopped off.'

'I would hate to be responsible for that!' He smiled. 'Perhaps it will be all right for me to assist you in the circumstances. Let me see if I understand correctly. You wish to know the names of those who have recently bought several bottles of Laphroaig malt, possibly a case?'

'In one. And to pin down the person, he may well have bought some Pommard burgundy at the same time.'

'We sell quite a lot of that. Of course, there are few superlative Pommards, but most will agree, many distinguished ones. Mussy is my favoured grower. Ninety was a very good year . . .'

Metcalfe listened with growing impatience to a long encomium of the wine's qualities, decided not to mention the Lanson in case further verbal flood gates were opened.

Eventually the owner said he'd look through the records. He walked to the end of the counter and then through a doorway into the small office beyond. When he returned, he said: 'Most strange.'

'How's that?'

'Only four customers have recently bought Laphroaig and only one a case. As the chance to enjoy the fine things of life widens, if seems fewer wish to enjoy that chance. So sad.'

'Did any of the four also have the wine?'

'The one who bought the case did.'

'What's his name?'

'Mr Tobin.'

Eureka! 'Does he come here often?'

'I think it would be correct to say, fairly frequently.'

'And buys a lot?'

'His purchases are certainly generous.'

'How much would he have spent in the past year?'

'I should have to examine the accounts closely to determine that.'

'Have a guesstimate.'

'I really find it very difficult.'

'You won't be locked up if you're wrong!'

'Perhaps between three and four thousand pounds. One imagines he entertains a great deal.'

'Does he use one of those credit cards that's so grand it'll buy you a Bentley if you want one?'

'We do not accept credit or debit cards.'

This had to be the last shop in the town, perhaps the county, where cards were viewed with suspicion. 'So it's cheque or cash?'

'Most customers settle their accounts by cheque.'

'As Tobin did?'

'I seem to remember he did not wish to have an account, although I naturally offered him that facility, and always paid in cash.'

Had Tobin been careful not to pay by card or cheque because both payments could be easily traced; had he, to save himself time and trouble, overlooked the danger of buying locally? 'Thanks for all your help and rest assured none of your customers – clients – will ever know you gave it.'

As Metcalfe walked back to his car, the sense of

satisfaction faded, to be replaced by one of bitterness. No DC could afford to run a home, maintain a wife and son, and spend that sort of money on booze. Surely the Wyatt family wouldn't knowingly have funded his drinking? It was beginning to seem likely that Tobin had been the canary he had been named.

The sun was low, but the evening still warm as Metcalfe parked in the yard of Bray's Cottage. He walked along to the wooden gate, around the house, and as he approached the front door, Charlotte opened it. Isser came bounding out, sniffed his trousers, and appeared to be about to cock a leg. He hastily moved.

'I hope you understand that's just being friendly?' she said.

'As the Stone Age priest used to kiss a beautiful female sacrifice before cutting her throat?'

'I imagine the motive was more mixed than Isser's . . . Come on in and have a drink. Or would you think it's still warm enough to play at being in Monte Carlo and sit outside?'

'Outside would be fine.'

'Good . . . You'll find a deckchair just beyond the corner, which is a sun-trap when there's not a south-westerly wind; go and sit after you've told me what you'd like.'

'May I have a gin and tonic?'

She smiled quickly. 'You may.' She returned inside, followed by Isser.

He walked along the brick path, around the corner of the house, and found the deckchair set on the grass. He sat. Facing him was a pond, some ten feet wide, the water murky where it was not covered in duckweed: he remembered Gwen's telling him that in the period when houses such as Bray's Cottage had been built, the clay for the bricks had sometimes been dug on site, which was why there were many ponds close to the buildings. Movement caught his attention and he identified a newt before it slid into the water, causing slight ripples. In a rough semicircle on the far side of the pond were pollarded ash trees, recently cut back to keep their growth in check, and a pigeon landed on the top branch of one, almost immediately taking off with a sharp clap of wings on identifying him as a potential danger. From the woods to his left, only just visible because of the lie of the land, he heard the raucous, arrogant call of a cock pheasant, warning off any would-be intruder that fancied its harem. A slight puff of cloud drifted overhead, casting a moving shadow across the fields. This, he thought, was balm for anyone who fought crime, and because of his experiences was ready to believe that while for the innocent there was a limit to happiness, there was none to frightened fear and despair.

Charlotte came round the house, in her right hand a silver salver on which were a tumbler, a wine glass, and a small dish of crisps. 'Hold on to this for a moment, will you, while I find another deckchair.'

He came to his feet. 'Let me get it.'

'You know from where?' she asked with light mockery.

'You can tell me.'

'But won't, since it's in the middle of a jumble and my mother said that if a man sees you live in a jumble, he'll get the wrong impression.'

'About what exactly?'

'She never explained.'

He took the salver from her, watched her walk away. Age so often damaged a figure, but hers had suffered little. She moved with a natural grace. She went out of sight and, careful to keep the salver horizontal, he

172

sat. Isser did not follow her, but came and stood in front of him, beseeching eyes and a partially opened, salivating mouth making it clear what was expected. He picked out a crisp and offered it. It was snatched from his hand.

Charlotte reappeared, a folded deckchair in her right hand; with easy efficiency, she opened it out and set it up without any of the usual confloptions. 'Would you like to pass me the wine before I sit? . . . No, don't move, reach out.'

He handed her the wineglass and crisps; she settled on the deckchair. Isser was about to jump up onto her lap when she said, 'No'; he hesitated, crossed to Metcalfe and stood, tail wagging.

'He's asking for a crisp, but don't give him one because he's too fat already.'

'My fingers are sealed.'

She drank. 'I seem to remember that the last time we met, you said you'd soon be retiring – but I imagine you haven't yet, since you're here.'

'I retired towards the end of March.'

'This is a social visit?'

'I took that risk.'

'I'm sorry you thought it could be a risk.'

She seemed as genuinely glad to see him again, as he to see her. He suffered self-contempt because he was lying.

'Are you enjoying retirement?'

'It's not the fun I hoped it would be. Days can become very long.'

'Have you no hobbies?'

'I used to collect stamps, but when I moved to CID there never seemed to be the time to continue.'

'First too little, then too much. Life in a nutshell.'

He said, uncertainly: 'Is something wrong?'

'Why do you ask?'

'You sound . . . rather down.'

'A not uncommon occurrence, as surely you must know.'

'And how! When there's no one to talk to, joke with, argue with, loneliness can grab one by the throat.'

'Are you an argumentative man?'

'When I know nothing about a subject, I'll argue over it from dawn to dusk.'

She smiled. 'You're far too sensible to act like that.' She fed Isser a crisp.

'I thought that was verboten.'

'What's the point of a rule if one doesn't have the pleasure of breaking it from time to time?'

Would she argue that what was the point of honesty if one didn't lie from time to time?

She invited him to stay for supper and he quickly accepted. Towards the end of the meal, he said: 'How's Mrs Tobin bearing up?'

'Not too badly.' She began to fiddle with the stem of her wineglass, looked quickly at him, then away. 'In your job, you must have had to deal with all sorts of people?'

'The whole gamut.'

'And understood how their minds worked?'

'I tried to, but very often didn't succeed; people do things which seem totally illogical and one can't begin to understand why they do them – sometimes I'm sure they don't know either . . . Is there a reason for asking?'

'Not really.' She drank. 'Yes, there is. I simply can't think how . . .'

'What?'

'How Victoria can be so emotionally divided. She's

built up a memory of Frank which would have one believing he was on the path to beatification. Yet after what happened . . .'

'What did happen?'

She didn't speak for several seconds. Then did not answer the question. 'Serena thinks she's painting a false picture for Leo's sake – he'll grow up believing his father was great.'

'Isn't that a good thing?'

'It would be if I didn't wonder if she's really trying to compensate for her sense of guilt.'

'Guilt in respect of what?'

'His death.'

'How could she bear the slightest responsibility for that?'

'Because some women can be so self-sacrificing, they believe they must be at least partially responsible for their husband's faults . . . Why the hell am I talking to you like this?'

'You are obviously worried and need to discuss the problem.'

'It'll probably sort itself out. Victoria's going out with Roger again.'

'An ex-boyfriend?'

'Yes.'

'You think that's wrong?'

'One could suggest it is a little soon after Frank's death, but as I said to Serena – who agreed – she's due some happiness and Roger's far more likely to give her that since they're from the same background . . . I'm sorry. That probably sounds incredibly snobby.'

Because she had no difficulty in guessing his background?

She stared directly at him. 'Similar backgrounds can

be important, not for their social values but because they usually provide a similar range of interests and that really matters in relationships after the first rush is over. I always placed her marriage to Frank as basically a two-fingered salute at family, friends, and the life she'd been brought up in . . . Tell me something I've often wondered – was he popular?'

'No. And it wasn't just a case of rank, as unpopularity often is.'

'What then?'

'He was always so keen to remind the lads how well off he was.'

'He believed that mattered?'

'In his own mind, he was one up because it made people jealous of him. On the odd occasion when he asked one of us along for a drink, it wasn't from friendship, it was to show he lived in a house none of us would ever be able to afford; when he and the family went on an expensive holiday, he was proving what a great life he led because he'd married a wealthy woman.'

'I think you're wronging him there.'

'Why?'

'As far as I know, Victoria has only relatively little money of her own, left to her by an aunt. Simon bought the house so she had a good start to her marriage, but after that he would have left her to stand on her own two feet because that's the way he thinks things should be. There's a touch of the Victorian paterfamilias in him.'

'Perhaps he decided he was being too harsh and relented and gave her a generous allowance.'

'What makes you think he might have done?'

'As I've said, Frank had luxurious tastes which he couldn't have met on his wage. When they went to the

West Indies last summer, it was a long way from a cheapie package holiday.'

'I suppose Serena might have given Victoria money on the quiet. But it would be unlike her to do anything she knew Simon would disagree with.'

He changed the conversation before she might wonder if he had some unspoken interest in Tobin's finances.

He looked at his watch. 'It's after eleven. I must move.'

'How the time can sometimes fly. An added bonus for your dropping in.'

He stood, crossed to the ancient panelled door, pulled the leather thong which activated the wooden bar on the outside, went through to the hall.

She remained in the doorway of the sitting room as he crossed to the front door. 'Come and see me the next time you're passing,' she said.

'I most certainly will.'

As he walked to his car, his thoughts were bitter. She had said that Victoria was emotionally divided – no more so than he. On the one hand, he was enjoying Charlotte's company more and more, on the other, he was using their growing relationship to question her without her realizing this because he lacked the courage to tell her the truth since to do so must affect their friendship.

Nineteen

Since Acton was out, Metcalfe went along the corridor to the CID general room. Seal was the only occupant.

'So how's the world when there's nothing to do and all the time to do it in?' Seal asked.

'Not as enjoyable as when there's plenty to do and only just enough time in which to do it.'

'If you're saying work's a pleasure, you must have been hitting the booze really hard.'

'When you reach my age, the fourth drink takes too much out of one to continue . . . Any idea where the Guv'nor is?'

'None at all. He's like a blue-arsed fly in perpetual motion. Must be wearing himself out and if he makes fifty without being boxed, he'll be lucky.'

'More likely he'll be sitting in the chief constable's chair.'

'You think he'll make the top job?'

'If not in this county, in another.'

'Then just so long as it's in a different force from the one I'm in . . . Have you heard the latest on the home front?'

'Not knowing what that is, can't tell.'

'A couple of days back, a report came in of a knocking shop on the outskirts of Barklestone where under-ages were providing the entertainment. A raid was mounted, but the report proved to be wrong and everyone at work was old enough to consider three times twenty-three old hat. Alf said some of the things the customers had been enjoying, you wouldn't believe.'

'He's quite right. I wouldn't.'

'He found three of 'em . . .'

At the conclusion of a long and detailed description, Metcalfe said: 'Alf suffers from an engorged imagination.'

'He swore it was fact.'

'He'd still claim he could walk on water when he was ten feet under.'

'One of the other lads there told me . . .' Seal became silent as Acton hurried into the room.

'Where's Sergeant Crowe?' Acton asked sharply.

'He went out half an hour ago, sir,' Seal replied.

'To where?'

'I can't say.'

'Why not?'

'He didn't mention it to me.'

'Find him and tell him to report to me.' Acton hurried out of the room, calling out as he did so: 'I want a word, Metcalfe.'

When certain he could not be overheard, Seal said: 'How the hell am I to get hold of the skipper when I've no idea where he is?'

'By bringing out the crystal ball.'

Metcalfe left and went along to the detective inspector's room. Acton was reading a report, pencil held ready to write corrections and sarcastic queries. He looked up. 'Have you made any progress?'

'The off-licence in town has identified Frank as someone who regularly spent a small fortune on booze.'

Acton put down the pencil.

'Added to everything else, that makes his lifestyle well beyond what his salary could begin to provide. Since there might have been a source of money through his wife, I had a word with Miss Wyatt – Mrs Tobin's paternal aunt. I put the questions as obliquely as possible and I'm reasonably certain she didn't realize I was asking them. She doubts her brother made Victoria an allowance and obviously the two women are on sufficiently good terms to expect she would have known if her brother had. She reckons her brother gave them the house as a marriage present and thereafter expected them to stand on their own two feet. She accepts Mrs Wyatt might have helped out on the quiet, but didn't think she would have done so, knowing her husband would object.'

'An unusual wife for this day and age. All that is opinion only – she's no certain knowledge?'

'Not as I gathered things to be.'

'Not solid enough to negate the possibility that one of the parents helped the daughter out financially if Tobin wasn't earning what he spent.'

'Which is why I need to question Victoria Tobin. It seems Tobin's death can't be weighing all that heavily because she's seeing an old boyfriend . . . Which makes it odd that she's building up Frank's memory as hard as apparently she is; I wonder if there's something that's not yet come to light? . . . So she shouldn't get too distressed if I have a chat. If I can't learn anything from her, I'll speak to the parents and try to find out if either of them did provide extra money.'

'Which inevitably will lead them to suspect you think Tobin was guilty of something.'

'I questioned Miss Wyatt without her realizing that fact.'

'Wyatt will be a lot sharper and he's likely to start raising hell.'

'Sir, we have to know one way or the other. If Tobin was crook, then we have to look at his death again because it becomes likely he sold duff information to someone and that someone became very aggrieved.'

'PM evidence bears out accidental death.'

'It wasn't that definite. It left room for assault.'

'An assault with feathers? You imagine a villain wouldn't have left Tobin obviously smashed up?'

'He was so drunk that even a light blow could have sent him sprawling. There's no fun in duffing up someone who doesn't know he's being duffed.'

'A villain looking for revenge would put his boot in, many times.'

'Tobin's knuckles bore signs of abrasions. Maybe he did so much damage, his assailant had cleared off before he collapsed.'

'Make your mind up – was he jelly or was he concrete?'

There was a silence.

'If I had a word with Victoria Tobin . . .' Metcalfe began.

'Do you know your Donne?'

'Who?'

'Any officer's betrayal diminishes the rest of us.'

'I don't quite follow, sir.'

'I told you at the beginning, this investigation had to be so low key it was next to invisible. If the news becomes public that a detective had been, or even might have been, working with criminals, the media would be on to the story like a shoal of piranhas. If you're not as smart as you think yourself and Mr Wyatt understands what you're after, if we re-open the question of Tobin's death and someone wonders why, the piranhas will be tearing us to bits.'

181

'Surely the possibility of bad publicity isn't more important than uncovering the truth?'

'The truth is, there is no proof, only ambiguous circumstantial evidence that Tobin was an informer.'

'And much of that ambiguity, maybe all, could be removed by talking to Mr and Mrs Wyatt and Victoria Tobin.'

'Tobin's dead.'

'And?'

'If he was bent, he can do no more harm now.'

'And we accept that as reason for closing down, leaving his murderer to laugh?'

'The evidence makes that scenario very unlikely.'

'Only if we close both eyes. But you reckon that's the way forward because otherwise there's the chance of your earning a career-killing black mark on your flimsy, even though you weren't in command at the time.'

'Have you finished?'

'Just one question. Does anyone still remember the old adage, "Justice is truth, truth is justice"?'

'Even in the short time you've worked for me, it's become very clear why you failed to gain any promotion. An inability to see the whole picture rather than one small dot in a corner, a sanctimonious, priggish belief that you alone are an arbiter of law and justice leave you unfit even to be a detective constable . . . Since there now is sufficient evidence for me to make a report to the chief constable, there is no call for you to continue the investigation. Present your final account as soon as possible . . . Your temporary warrant card.' Acton held out his hand.

Metcalfe brought the plastic holder out of his pocket, extracted the warrant card, threw it down onto the desk. A juvenile gesture but, very briefly, a satisfying one.

Twenty

As he turned off the road and into the oak-lined drive, Metcalfe swore. Acton's words haunted him. Was his regard for the truth sanctimonious and priggish? Was he a fool because he believed so firmly that when truth was denied, justice suffered, when justice suffered, chaos crept nearer?

He brought the car to a halt by the side of the colour-filled, raised circular flower bed, crossed to the portico and the massive front door, activated the knocker. When Enid opened the door, he asked if the Wyatts were in.

'No, they ain't.' Her sharp curiosity was immediate.

'Do you know where they are?'

'Gone on a holiday; them and Mrs Tobin and little Leo.'

'When will they be back?'

'Mrs Wyatt said they was to be away several weeks.' She decided she needed to assure him that the house would be well guarded and explained at length that she would be coming in every day, even at the weekends, to make certain all was well; and John, the gardener, he'd be around . . .

He thanked her, returned to his car feeling thoroughly deflated. Having, after much internal argument, made up his mind on moral grounds that he must continue the investigation, ignoring the fact Acton had declared it closed and that he would be unauthorized and unpaid, he was now forced to accept his high-minded resolution had become meaningless. No Wyatts, no further investigation.

When he reached the end of the drive and turned left, it was on the unformulated assumption he'd return home. But even as he accelerated through the gears, he decided the empty house could only exacerbate his present mood of depression. He needed diversion – a drive through the countryside to the sea to watch the ships that plied the Channel, or perhaps to the Duke and Duchess, a pub deep in the heart of nowhere which had not been redecorated in a decade and offered a dingy welcome that made so desirable a change from the theme pubs and their schmaltz . . .

By chance – so he assured himself – he chose a route which passed through Ronefield. The nearer he was to the village, the more certain he became that the quiet warmth of friendliness was to be preferred to the artificial bonhomie of a pub . . .

As he approached the wooden gate, Isser bounded up to the other side and barked a welcome. He opened the gate, bent down and stroked Isser before continuing along the path. Charlotte was wearing crimson-coloured slacks; one of the few older women, he decided, who could wear slacks and not look like the model for a saucy seaside postcard. 'I was passing and decided to test your open-ended invitation. Hope I haven't arrived when you were about to go out?'

'I was, but only because it would give me something to do. I suggest we sit indoors today because the wind's surprisingly sharp. I'll make some coffee.'

He followed her into the house, was told to go into the sitting room while she went through to the kitchen.

When he sat, Isser jumped on to his lap and demanded attention. In the room, there was a faint smell which triggered memories he could not immediately place; then he noticed the platted lavender posy in a silver mug on one of the small occasional tables and he remembered the bunches of dried lavender, bound with silk ribbon, which his mother had used to make.

Charlotte, carrying a tray, entered. She put the tray down. 'Black or white coffee, sugar or saccharin, brandy snap or chocolate digestive?'

'Black with a dash, two level teaspoonfuls of sugar, and a chocolate digestive, please.'

'A man who knows precisely what he wants! I have a friend who takes five minutes to decide whether to have coffee and then another ten on how much sugar . . . Don't stand, I'll bring the things over.' She carried the tray across. 'Your cup and saucer are the ones nearer to you.'

Isser, who had remained on his lap, hurriedly rose to a somewhat precarious sitting position and eyed the biscuits.

'He's not to have one, however much he asks,' she said.

He lifted up the cup and saucer from the tray, had to try to reach around Isser with his free hand to help himself to a biscuit.

'Put him down on the floor.'

'He seems very reluctant to leave.'

'He has a passion for chocolate biscuits and would eat a whole tin of them if given half a chance . . . Isser, get down.' Isser ignored her. 'Will you get down?' He looked with even greater desire at the biscuit held beyond his reach.

She put the tray down, lifted Isser off Metcalfe's lap.

185

'I thought of taking him to obedience classes, but when I had a word with the instructor, he was perfectly honest and said I'd probably be wasting my time because the true Lakie will never do what it doesn't want to.'

'That's half the breed's charm.'

'Disobedience is admirable?'

'In dogs and DCs.'

'Why do you say that?'

'Because I wasn't thinking.'

'Thinking but, I suspect, not about what you were saying.'

'Just not thinking.'

She crossed to an armchair, sat.

'I called in at Bredgley Hall earlier on,' he said.

'For any particular reason?'

'To ask a couple of questions.'

'I thought you'd retired?'

'County HQ have suddenly demanded further details about one of the reports I made.'

'This long afterwards?'

'The mills of bureaucracy grind slowly. Although I wouldn't admit to authority, I've forgotten some of the facts and was hoping Mr or Mrs Wyatt would be able to refresh my memory. But the daily said they were away with Mrs Tobin and her son.'

'My brother had one of his I-know-what's-best-for-everyone revelations and decided the family must have a complete change of scenery. He's always imagined himself crewing a clipper – nothing is more unlikely since he can't stand being cold and wet, or living on weevil-infested biscuits – so when he read that the first square-rigger in virtually a century had been built and was cruising with a limited number of passengers who would enjoy luxurious conditions, he booked the family

186

on a voyage. So now they're somewhere on the seven seas, watching men haul, brace, and doing whatever else one does on it.'

'Her. A ship is always feminine.'

'Would you know why?'

'I have heard an explanation.'

'Tell.'

'The more screws she has, the faster she moves.'

'Only a male could believe that!' She fed Isser a piece of biscuit.

'Breaking the rules again?'

'You can't expect me to be so cruel as to go on ignoring his desperate appeal . . . Perhaps I can help you with whatever it is you want to ask Simon?'

'Thanks for the offer, but I doubt it. County HQ will just have to wait to have the report detailed to their satisfaction.'

'Has something changed?'

'In what way?'

'You told me Frank's death had been classified an accident, yet you're still making enquiries . . . ?'

'Just wrapping up some loose ends.'

'It will be a tremendous relief when they're wrapped and it's really all over.'

'I'm sure it will. Is Mrs Tobin . . .'

'Is she what?'

'It's none of my business.'

'When you were still working, you seemed to think everything was your business!'

'I'm afraid it was my job to be very, very curious.'

'Don't ever let Simon know I told you this, but he once said you were like a Peeping Tom, trying to peer at things you shouldn't be looking at . . . Now tell me what you started to ask.'

'Is she still seeing her ex?'

'I gather she was reluctant to go on the cruise and refused to say why. Simon complained she was being stupid and sea air was just what she needed. He seemed surprised when I pointed out that whereas sea air will merely promote sea sickness, Roger can give her the kind of support and reassurance she needs.'

'Reassurance as to what?'

'Isn't that obvious? That the loss of a partner doesn't have to mean the end of enjoying life.'

'A very hard lesson to learn.'

'A bloody hard lesson, but one that has to be learnt.'

'I was wondering . . . ?'

'That seems to be a habit of yours.'

'Would you like to have a meal somewhere?'

'I can't think of a better idea.'

As May shaded into June and the weather remained warm and sunny, they saw each other frequently. They had picnics, driving to areas of the countryside one or other, or both, hardly knew; they took the ferry to Boulogne and discovered a restaurant where the grubby exterior belied the Lucullan food served inside and they returned there on subsequent trips despite her expressed fear that soon she would be having to let out the seams of all her clothes; they spent evenings in each other's home; and there arose an acceptance, not hinted at in words, yet acknowledged by looks, gestures, momentary tension, that they would share a bed, but not just yet – life had taught them to approach pleasure slowly because if one rushed, it might prove ephemeral.

The fifteenth of June was a cloudless hot day and as he drove from Setonhurst to Ronefield, Metcalfe tried to remember a poem (by whom?), in which the poet had declared what bliss it was to be alive (had there been some mention of dawn?). That was exactly how he felt.

He turned off the main road, drove along a winding lane, through a village which lodged on a small rise, and along a straight stretch of road that was reputed to be of Roman origin. On the skyline to his left was the small stand of poplars which marked the side lane that would take him down to Bray's Cottage. He enjoyed an excited expectancy which recalled the time he had been courting Gwen. He was surprised how he could now think of Gwen and not feel he was being a traitor to her memory; on the contrary, he was certain she would have understood and approved.

In the small yard, he switched off the engine and climbed out of the Fiesta. Excited barks announced Isser was on the other side of the wooden gate into the garden; when he was halfway to the gate, this was opened and Isser rushed up to him and demanded to be picked up and fondled. Charlotte met him as he entered the garden and kissed him.

'I swear he heard your car as you turned into our lane,' she said. 'He was barking at least a minute before you drove in.'

'Just as well I wasn't trying to make a surreptitious approach.'

'And why would you be doing that?'

'Give me time and I'll think of an answer.'

She linked her arm with his. 'I've had an idea.'

'Do I hold my breath?'

'The family returns tomorrow. Let's run over after lunch and leave them the small welcome back present I've bought.'

'Fine.'

'Is it? You hardly sound enthusiastic.'

He wasn't. To visit Bredgley Hall was to be forced to acknowledge something which, from pride, he tried to keep hidden from himself – she was from a wealthy background and must have considerable money of her own. By comparison, a DC's pension was stale peanuts. Class distinctions were said to have become blurred where they hadn't disappeared; if so, their place had been taken by financial distinctions. 'I was being nosy and wondering what the present could be,' he said, prevaricating.

'A Dawson print of a square rigger under full sail. Come and look at it and see if you approve.' She led the way into the house.

In the sitting room, she picked up a loosely wrapped flat parcel, undid the brown paper, and rested the framed print on its base as she held it upright. 'Well?'

'Very romantic when seen from ashore.'

'There speaks common sense!' She laid the print flat and rewrapped it in the brown paper. 'I must check the joint. I'm cooking a piece of entrecôte – something I like, but seldom have because it needs to be a reasonably sized joint not to become dry in the cooking, and being on my own, it would be cold meat for days. Two people can't really live as cheaply as one, but they can certainly enjoy more variety when it comes to eating. There's the latest *Country Life* on the table. I won't be long.' She left, followed by Isser.

He ignored the magazine – the advertisements of houses for sale were designed to make one dissatisfied – and crossed to the window and looked out at the lawn, hedge, and narrow field beyond. Soon, they would live together; would it be as man and wife? Liaisons were so common these days, little or no social kudos was lost by enjoying one; and she might prefer to keep her independence. Her brother would surely far prefer a marriage. He corrected his thoughts. Her brother would probably prefer no relationship after the previous experience of his daughter's alliance with a policeman . . .

'Alec,' she called out.

He went into the hall and through to the kitchen, where she was spooning some of the contents of a tin into a dog bowl. 'Would you like to be an angel?'

'I'm not already one?'

'From what I was taught when young, I hope not.'

He laughed. Occasionally, she made a comment which told him that her certainty about the future matched his. 'How do I qualify as a temporary angel?'

'By laying the table. The meat's cooking faster than I wanted and we'll have to eat fairly soon – there's nothing worse than overdone beef.'

He went through to the dining room, as heavily beamed as the sitting room and with a slightly smaller fireplace that lacked an inglenook. On the table was half a loaf on a breadboard. He picked up the breadboard and carried it into the kitchen.

'Oh, my God! I forgot to finish clearing the table when Marie rang and insisted on talking for hours.' Isser began to bark. 'Stop suggesting you've been starved for days . . . Have I left anything else on the table?'

'Only some crumbs, and if you'll give me a duster, I'll get rid of them.'

She brought a handful of biscuit out of a pack, dropped it into the dog bowl, put that down on the floor. Isser ate as if he had, in truth, been starving. 'What it is to invite one's guest to clear up one's breakfast remains!'

'I hope I'm not still regarded as a guest?'

'No, Alec, far from that.' Her tone expressed what words did not.

'Good. So where's the duster?'

'In there.' She pointed at the middle built-in cupboard against the inner wall.

He opened the cupboard door and bent down to look inside. On the top shelf was a square container in which were several pieces of material and he brought the top one out.

'Is that the best you can find?' she asked. 'There should be some proper dusters.'

'This will do since it's only to clear up some crumbs.'

He returned into the dining room and used the rag to sweep crumbs into his left hand. As he straightened, it struck him that there was something familiar about the colouring of the material which, he now judged, was part of an old shirt. Perhaps he had a shirt of similar pattern? He returned to the kitchen, dropped the crumbs into the bucket under the sink, put the rag back in the cupboard.

'There's time for one drink, so what would you like?'

'The usual, please.'

'I'll have a G and T as well. Will you pour them? There's a lemon somewhere, but I don't know exactly where.'

He laughed.

'Thank you very much for that! For your information, I'm not as scatterbrained as you obviously think. It's just that I've had a heavy morning.'

'Now made heavier?'

'If you're looking for a compliment, you're out of luck. Suppose you get the drinks while I lower the heat under the peas.'

In the sitting room, Isser jumped on her lap and tried to wipe his mouth on her blouse; she pushed him away. 'What shall we do this afternoon after we've dropped the print at Bredgley Hall?'

'According to the local rag, Estor Castle is open to the public on Wednesdays and Saturdays. Have you been there?'

'Not for a very long time and I'd like to go again. The castle was in the news last week – did you read about it?'

'No.'

'An expert in ancient buildings was looking around and came across something in the dungeons which convinces him that at least a part of the castle dates back a century before contemporary thinking holds.'

'Maybe it was a prisoner's comments scratched on a stone before he was taken off to be racked.'

'I hope it's something very different; it's awful when pain provides a memory. They were so terribly cruel in those days.'

'No crueller than people can be these days.'

'When you were working, did you understand why someone became like that?'

'No.'

'Could you tell if someone had a beastly nature?'

'No, again. We had a case of appalling cruelty to animals and the culprit was a man who oozed friendly charm. He put that to such good effect that the judge listened to his story and gave him so short a sentence, he was outside almost before he went inside. Probably, he went straight back to torturing animals because that lets him think what a powerful man he is.'

'Is that why he was cruel?'

'It's my interpretation. He enjoyed what many would call a privileged life so I couldn't think of any other reason why he should . . .' He stopped.

'What did he do?'

'I'd much rather not tell you.'

'And I think I'd much rather not hear.' She called Isser to her and fondled his ears for a while before she picked up her glass and drained it. 'I'll start dishing.'

'Can I help?'

'You can come and talk to me and stop my thinking about the bastards who hurt animals.'

It was while he was driving home, just after eleven that night, he suddenly realized why the pattern of the piece of shirt had seemed vaguely familiar.

Twenty-One

H e entered divisional HQ and made his way along the
ground floor to the Exhibits Room. It was locked,
as it should be but often wasn't. He went up one floor to
the front room. The duty PC was an occasional drinking
companion, the sergeant a morose man who seemed to enjoy
being difficult; both were talking to members of the public.
By good luck, the middle-aged woman was the first to leave.
Metcalfe went up to the counter and spoke to the PC.

'Beats me what you're doing here! Get paid a lovely
pension and all you can think of doing is rush back to
work,' the PC said.

'It's called enthusiasm.'

'It's called bloody stupidity . . . So is there something
you want?'

'The key to Exhibits.'

The PC turned and went into the small room beyond
the counter, returned with a labelled key. 'The book's by
the sarge . . .'

'There's no call for that – you'll have the key back in
half a jiffy.'

'Just so long as old George doesn't know it's not been
signed in and out.' He indicated the sergeant, who was
talking to an elderly man who was clearly trying his
patience. 'The silly sod's going on and on about doing
everything by the book.'

Once inside the Exhibits Room, Metcalfe checked the

tiers of shelving which ran along three walls and quickly found the container marked 'Tobin'. He brought this down and placed it on the central table, lifted out the few items. The collar was in a transparent plastic bag on the label of which were the relevant details. The thin red and green check pattern, on a light background, looked identical. But because he wanted to believe himself mistaken, he brought the collar out and used a small ruler to measure the distance, vertical and horizontal, between colours.

He returned to the front room, handed the key back to the PC.

'You want something?' the sergeant demanded from the far end of the counter as the elderly man turned away and walked towards the outer door.

'A warm welcome,' Metcalfe replied.

'According to what I've heard, you're no longer on temporary duty?'

'Never believe rumours.'

'Which means you've no right of access. So where have you just been, doing what?'

'Checking on something.'

'Suppose I decide there needs to be a report?'

'You'll have to spend much time filling in forms and while you're doing that, you'll curse yourself for having been so pedantic.'

The sergeant reluctantly decided there was much sense in what had just been said. Sullen-faced, he walked the length of the counter, lifted the end flap, crossed to a doorway, and passed through.

'They say his old woman's sourer than him, but that's impossible,' remarked the PC.

'Never underestimate the female's ability to outshine the male.'

*   *   *

Metcalfe braked the car to a halt, switched off the engine, climbed out. In the sharp sunshine, surrounded by green lawns, flowers, and fields, backed by woods, Bray's Cottage was, if on a smaller scale, as much an epitome as Bredgley Hall of all that was best about the British countryside.

As he walked down to the gate, he assured himself he was acting for Charlotte's benefit. He wished he could believe that. Isser was barking and he found himself silently shouting, 'Shut up.' Before he opened the gate, he looked back at the road, fearing he might see her drive in, even though she'd told him she was having lunch with an old school friend and wouldn't be back until well into the afternoon. For the first time, he fully understood how conscience could wreck a novice's crime.

When he had seen where she left the front door key, he'd warned her that that was one of the obvious places where a casual thief would look; he hoped she'd ignored his advice either to take the key with her or find a far more secure hiding place – his housebreaking skills were not great. The key was still under the flower pot and he thanked her misguided casualness.

He unlocked and opened the front door. Isser came out at speed, barked several times, demanded and received attention, then wildly chased an imaginary fox. As he crossed the lawn and wriggled through the low hedge, Metcalfe suffered the fear that he'd continue on, to end up in the middle of the woods, bedraggled, lost . . . He shouted 'Isser!' several times, whistled furiously. He had all but given up hope and was preparing to set off into the woods when Isser returned. Metcalfe thankfully guided him indoors.

In the kitchen, Metcalfe opened the middle cupboard and brought out the container in which were kept the dusters and rags. Initially there was no sign of the section of shirt he'd used to clear the breadcrumbs from the dining-room table and he had just come to the thankful conclusion that for one reason or another it had been discarded and he'd never be able to be certain, when he found it at the bottom. He spread it out on one of the working surfaces. Resignedly, he measured the check pattern; all the measurements matched those of the collar exactly.

He said goodbye to Isser, locked the front door, replaced the key under the flower pot. He vainly wished that Charlotte had cleared the dining-room table before his arrival.

He stared at the television, but if asked what was showing would not have been able to answer. The facts circled in his mind. The collar in Tobin's house had been torn from a shirt; in Charlotte's house was part of that shirt. When a witness had identified the car outside Tobin's house that Tuesday evening as belonging to Wyatt, Charlotte had provided an alibi for her brother which had negated the identification . . . If she had been lying because Wyatt had been in Tobin's house . . .

Because he wanted to deny such conclusion, he tried to accept the possibility of coincidence, but failed. Wyatt was involved. Why? What would have caused him to drive to Athin Road at that time of night to confront his son-in-law? There had been a physical argument – what could the argument have been about?

A sergeant instructor at the college where he'd done his preliminary training, whose abilities had owed far more to experience than theory, had often said that the key to many a crime was something – presence, absence, action, inaction, regularity, irregularity – which caused a blip in what one would expect to be the normal sequence of events. Victoria and Leo had not been sleeping in Athin Road the night of Tobin's death, but had been staying with a friend who lived not far away. Could one say it was unusual for a wife to take her child and leave her husband to spend the night nearby with a friend? Charlotte had described Victoria as painting the memory of a husband who deserved beatification. Might that be the reaction of a woman trying to conceal bitter truth from herself as well as her son, rather than coming to terms with it? Would the friend be able to answer some or any of the questions? What was her name? . . . Eventually, he remembered that – Hilary Pernell – but not the address and he went out to get the telephone directory.

Having been misdirected by a woman as she left the post office in the centre of the village, it took him time to find Hopstand, an imitation Georgian house two roads to the south of the traditional green, which had both duck-pond and cricket pitch.

Hilary was a blonde, of doubtful provenance. Her worry was immediate when he introduced himself. He said lightly: 'I only want to ask you a few questions.'

'But why . . . I mean . . .'

'Perhaps I might come in and explain?'

Flustered, she pushed the door wide open and stepped to one side. 'Would you like to go . . .' True to form, she did not finish the sentence, but a wave of her hand directed him into a sitting room that was in a muddle; newspaper pages, magazines, and a couple of books were spread out over chairs and an occasional table, on top of a video recorder were untidily heaped tapes, in a cut-glass vase a bunch of roses drooped and dropped their petals, on the floor in front of the fireplace was a very battered model revolver.

She sat, fiddled with the loose cover on the armchair. 'What do you want to know about?'

'It is in connection with the death of Frank Tobin.'

'I thought that that was, well . . .'

'I'm afraid there are still one or two questions which need to be answered.'

'But I don't know anything about it.'

'I'm sure that's right, Mrs Pernell, but I still have to ask you. Call it the tyranny of routine . . . Frank Tobin died on the night of the sixth of March. I understand that Mrs Tobin and her son were staying here with you?'

'Yes.'

'At what time did they arrive?'

'I can't remember. I really don't know because . . .'

Her nervousness had increased, not decreased, despite his friendly manner: she was taking care not to meet his gaze, but kept looking at the door and fidgeting with her dress. He judged it the moment to draw a long bow. 'You weren't expecting her, were you?'

'I don't understand why you're asking.'

'Your answer will help me clear up the last few remaining points of the case.'

'But I can't tell you.'

'Why is that?'

'I promised Vicky . . . I know I did tell her father, but I thought he just had to know, even if it was bound to upset him.'

'Did your news upset him?'

'Vicky's always said he has a quick temper. But wouldn't any father be . . .'

'Angry?'

'Suppose you learned your son-in-law had hit your daughter and grandson? How would you feel?'

'Furious.'

'What kind of a man behaves like that?' In a rush of words, she briefly spoke more coherently. 'Vicky tried to tell me that being drunk was an excuse. I didn't say anything because it would only have upset her more, but drink doesn't make a man nasty, it just releases the nastiness that's already in him. Wouldn't you agree?'

'Indeed. So when you learned what had happened, you phoned Mr Wyatt?'

'I didn't really know what to do, only that I had to do something.'

'And he told his sister?'

'I wouldn't know about that.'

'Has Mrs Tobin since mentioned any more about what happened that night?'

'All she ever says is what a wonderful man Frank was. How can she be so blind? She's always faced the truth before.'

'There can come a time when to do so is just too painful . . . Thanks for your help.'

'You won't . . . I mean, I did promise . . .'

'She'll learn nothing from me.'

That, he thought as he made his way to his car, had been a false assurance. The evidence must become public when the case finally reached court.

Twenty-Two

M etcalfe braked the Fiesta to a halt on the half-mile-long straight stretch of road that ran alongside the sea wall. He climbed out, locked the doors, crossed the pavement and climbed down the concrete steps to the shingle. The sea was in a quiet mood, each small wave breaking gently and briefly surging up the pebbles with a sushing noise, then retreating; the air was redolent with the ocean smell. Well out to sea, little more than a smudge on the horizon, were two large ships; much closer to land, a cabin cruiser was slicing through the water at speed, leaving a creaming wake.

He searched amongst the pebbles for those which were thin and almost flat. When young, he'd been able to skim a pebble along the surface of the sea up to a dozen times; now, after nine throws, his best was three. *Sic transit gloria mundi*, as his father had been so fond of saying, for no particular reason. He walked slowly on, twice having to skip a couple of feet shoreward as the surge of a wave reached further inland than had its predecessors.

He thought he had probably learned enough to surmise what had happened that night in March. Tobin had been drunk, a row between him and Victoria had escalated into physical assault, she had fled the house with Leo, unable to meet a situation for which her upbringing had not prepared her. Hilary, horrified to learn what had

202

happened, trying to help in typically haphazard manner, had phoned Wyatt; as furious as any father should be, he had driven to Athin Road to face Tobin, with disastrous results . . . How accurate was this scenario? How to make certain one way or the other? As he passed a man who sat on a small folding chair, waiting for a bell attached to the line of a fishing rod to ring, he was forced to accept the obvious answer.

Charlotte kissed him, then said as she stepped back: 'I phoned several times this morning and could only get your beastly answering machine. I was beginning to worry something had happened to you.'

Isser pawed his leg and he bent down to make a brief fuss of him. 'I had to go to the station and have a word with the DI to clear up something,' he said, as he straightened up.

'And that's a good excuse for not phoning me to decide where we'd have lunch, leaving me uncertain whether or not to prepare something here?'

'I'll be honest . . .' He paused, briefly conscious of the hypocrisy of those three words. 'I forgot because of the DI's sudden summons.'

'Since it was work, I'll generously forgive you on one condition, that we eat at the Thai restaurant I've been wanting to try for ages.'

They went into the sitting room and as she sat, Isser jumped onto her lap. When she failed to take immediate notice of him, he nibbled her wrist. 'You sound rather down in the dumps, Alec. Was it an unpleasant meeting with the detective inspector?'

He realized that by providing a false excuse, he had fortuitously placed himself in a position in which he could raise the question that had to be asked without her realizing his motive. 'Very unpleasant. He claimed fresh evidence in Frank's case had come to light.'

'What was that?'

'It's been suggested he was so drunk the night he died that he attacked Victoria and that's why she and Leo left home.'

She said fiercely: 'That's ridiculous. He was a rough diamond, but not a complete sod.'

'I told the DI it was very unlikely.'

'You should have said it was impossible. Frank would never have struck Victoria; do you understand, never.'

The vehemence with which she had spoken suggested she was scared – scared because a little of the truth had finally been dragged into the light?

'You must tell the detective inspector and make him understand.' She spoke more calmly.

'I did my best to do just that, but I didn't make any ground because he's convinced there's at least some truth in the story. Quite bluntly, there's nothing to be gained, and maybe something to be lost, by trying to pressure him.'

'How can he be so stupid? Vicky would be mortified if she knew anyone could possibly believe that.'

'I can imagine. And another thing, it would make nonsense of her beatifying Frank.'

'Do you have to sneer at her?'

'I'm only using words you said to me,' he answered quietly.

'I . . . I'm sorry, darling.'

It was the first time she had used that endearment. There was bitter irony because of the circumstances in which she had.

'It's all so . . . The family's been struggling to come to terms with the tragedy, then out of the blue you tell me

204

the detective inspector believes it possible Frank struck
Vicky and Leo.'

He hadn't mentioned Leo's being hit.

'It's all just too horrible. That he could begin to think
it possible . . .'

'Sadly, there is a lot of domestic violence.'

'But not in our kind of homes.'

She was lucky, or blind, to be able to believe that.

'Can you understand why I went for you a moment
ago?' she asked anxiously.

'Of course.' Understanding could be ambiguous.

Through the sitting-room window, the curtain half drawn,
Charlotte watched the tail lights of the Fiesta drive onto
the road and then disappear behind the hedge. She swore.
Isser, worried by her tone, stood close to her, head
cocked to one side, seeking reassurance that whatever
was wrong, it was not his fault. He was ignored. Tail
down, he wormed his way into the small space under
the nearer armchair, seeking sanctuary from unidenti-
fied peril.

She went into the hall and across to the phone on the
corner cupboard. Serena answered the call and for several
minutes, to her growing frustration, the conversation
was social.

'You'd like a word with Simon?' Serena finally asked.

'If I may.'

'I'll find him. Don't be surprised if he sounds like a
bear with a sore head – he's suffering from having spent
part of the afternoon trying to convince John that we don't
want another herbaceous border. John can be incredibly
stubborn.'

'Which is probably why he's such a good gardener.'

'I hadn't thought of that. But he does sometimes make

life so very difficult . . . Hang on and I'll find the lord and master – in his own estimation, that is.'

Two minutes later, Wyatt said: 'I'm glad you've phoned, Charlotte. Been meaning to tell you that one of the people we met on the cruise –'

She interrupted him. 'Can you speak freely?'

'Yes. Why?'

'Alec's just left. There's fresh evidence come to light.'

'What's he talking about? The case is closed.'

'Obviously, it isn't. The police now believe Frank may have attacked Vicky and Leo on the day he died.'

'God Almighty! That means . . . How the hell have they learned that?'

'He didn't explain.'

'Why didn't you ask?'

'Simon, start thinking. Of course I said it was utterly ridiculous. But if I'd shown too much concerned interest in why and how, he'd have wondered why I was so inquisitive and maybe would have started putting two and two together.'

'Didn't you tell him it was impossible?'

'I've just said I did.'

'Wouldn't he listen?'

'If you mean did I begin to convince him, I've no idea. It's difficult to read him if he doesn't want to be read.'

'Even when you've got to know him intimately well?'

'It's hardly the moment for snide and inaccurate remarks.'

'I thought it was all over. Now you suddenly tell me it isn't. What the hell do we do?'

'There's only one reasonable solution. You have to persuade Vicky that if she's asked, she denies Frank ever hit her.'

'I can't do that.'

'Why not?'

'She'll feel humiliated to learn I know.'

'Better her humiliated than you in jail.'

'I did not kill him—'

'For God's sake, Simon; you think you have to convince me? But look at things as the police will. Even if they eventually believe your version of events, they're going to accuse you of trying to upset justice by lying, aren't they? And me as well. Have you thought about the possibility they'll question Leo?'

'Shit!'

'Quite.'

'He may have forgotten all about it.'

'But he may not. And asking him to forget will make certain he tells everyone.'

'Maybe . . . maybe I should make a clean breast of everything.'

'Like a true, if somewhat delayed, gentleman? That'll blow everything wide open after we've done our damnedest to hush it all up.'

'We must do something.'

'There are times when it's better to do nothing . . . Let's look at things calmly. How are they going to prove Frank struck Vicky and Leo, providing the motive for your row with Frank? If Vicky denies anything and everything and Leo does pipe up he was hit, she can pass it off by saying he kept trying to put a finger in a light socket and Frank had to give him a tap to stop him and make him understand how dangerous that was . . . You just have to explain everything to Vicky.'

'What if she then talks to Serena?'

'You must persuade her not to.'

'But they've become even closer after Frank's death.'

'If the worst comes to the worst and she does blurt out

everything to Serena, at least it will be kept within the family.'

'It will upset Serena most terribly.'

'Better that than having the facts splashed all over the pages of the tabloids for Joe Soap to gloat over.'

'I wish . . .'

'Didn't you give up wishing when you realized Father Christmas was just an out-of-work actor?'

At sunrise on Saturday, the sky was lightly cloudy; by nine, it was cloudless and the day was already warm. Metcalfe finished his breakfast, cleared the table and put the various things in the washing-up machine. He carried on through to the hall, sat by the phone and for the next twenty minutes, using the authority he no longer possessed, requested phone companies to provide logs of calls made in February, March, and April, by Simon Wyatt. He then phoned divisional HQ and told Carter to hold all faxes addressed to him and to make certain Acton obtained no sight of them.

On Monday afternoon, Carter rang to say that two faxes had been received, one from BT – or whatever they now called themselves – and one from a mobile company. Metcalfe drove across to divisional HQ.

Carter, looking as if he'd been on a bender lasting days, was struggling with a computer. 'If they wanted us to be high-flying technics, they ought to pay us the proper wage for what we do.'

'Wouldn't you find that a considerable disadvantage?' Metcalfe sat on the corner of the desk. 'Thanks for organizing things – no possibility the Guv'nor got his nose near them?'

'Not so much as a sniff . . . What's it all in aid of?'

208

'I'm trying to find out if a call was made on a certain day at a time which could make it significant, especially if the two parties aren't regular phone correspondents.'

'If you can understand what that means, you're a better man than me. Is it still the Tobin case?'

'Kind of.'

'Never before met anyone who's retired, yet can't keep away from work.'

'It gets into the blood.'

'Then if I were you, I'd head down to the nearest hospital and ask for an immediate transfusion.' He pulled open the right-hand drawer of the desk and brought out several sheets of paper.

Metcalfe folded them, put them in his coat pocket.

'So how is life?' Carter asked.

'It jogs along. And for you?'

'Bloody chaos. You know what family life sometimes gets like . . .' He came to an abrupt stop, remembering that it was a long time since Metcalfe had known. Hurriedly, he said: 'Mary's well now, but we had a hell of a scare; thankfully, it turned out to be much less than it might have been. Joe's doing well at university and reckons he'll get at least a two one. As I said to him, "Don't start cackling before you've laid the egg."'

'Which he must have found rather confusing, being a man.'

'And Daisy! Sixteen and making her mother worry . . .'

Metcalfe was eager to leave, but owed Carter the favour of listening to a long complaint about a daughter who dressed appallingly, listened to a noise she claimed was music, went out with bad-mannered boys who obviously had only one aim in life . . .

The drive home took longer than usual, thanks to thick traffic, and it was past eleven when he settled in the front room, brought the faxes from his pocket, and studied them.

On his mobile, Wyatt had phoned Charlotte on the 6th of March at 2007 hours. That surely would have been before he reached Athin Road – if he had gone there? Telling his sister what he had learned from Hilary Pernell and asking her to provide an alibi if that proved necessary? If so, there was premeditation . . . Calls to Charlotte on the mobile were relatively infrequent. A small indication that the one on the 6th had been very important to him? On the 10th of March, four calls, at very short intervals, had been made to the same number in Inglewood; the first three had lasted less than a minute, the fourth slightly longer. It was a pattern which suggested sharp, even panicky need to contact someone. Because he had learned that the police suspected it had been his car parked outside Tobin's house at the relevant time on the Tuesday and the person to whom he was trying to speak had the potential to help?

He went into the hall, dialled inquiries, gave police identification and asked for the name and address of the subscriber to whom Wyatt had made those four calls.

Twenty-Three

Inglewood – originally named after woods which had been felled during the eighteenth and nineteenth centuries – was a small town which had escaped much development because it was well away from motorways, the railway had been axed decades before during the Beeching cuts, and light industry and large businesses found its location far less suitable than other and nearby towns; its roots still lay with the countryside.

Large houses to the south, set in generous gardens, were still occupied by sole owners and only one or two had been turned into flats or offices. No. 15 Eccles Road was an Edwardian house on three floors, in appearance symmetrical from a centre line. Metcalfe swung open the wrought-iron gate and walked the twenty feet along the gravel path, on either side of which was lawn, to the two steps which led up to the porch with imitation stained-glass side windows. He rang the bell. The door, newly painted in a deep Prussian blue, was opened by a woman of notable, muscular size and dressed without any apparent regard to appearance. Her features were marked by a scar that stretched from the corner of her mouth to the middle of her right cheek. She stared at him, said nothing.

'I'd like a word with Miss Ryan.'

'Don't know you.'

He didn't know her, but he knew her type; made tough and bitter by life and afraid of no one. Her sharp antagonism and the hard, calculating manner in which she regarded him provided the first indication of the nature of the household. 'I still want a word with Miss Ryan.'

'She ain't here.'

'Where is she?'

'Can't say.' She shut the door.

He rang the bell. He rang it a second and third time; the door was opened again. 'You want I call the police?' she demanded, her attitude suggesting that physical violence on her part was an alternative.

'Detective Constable Metcalfe.'

She stared hard and long at him. 'You ain't from local.'

'C Division.'

'Where's your warrant card?'

'At home.'

'Then get lost.'

'You'd rather I ask the locals to come here and vouch for me? Extra work always gets up their noses. I'm surprised you want to raise so much aggro that they'll start turning this place over.'

She chewed her lower lip, her anger expressed in her features. She kicked the door fully open, jerked her head in the direction of an open doorway to her right.

He went into a room that was furnished with taste; if some of the pieces of furniture were genuine, it was expensive taste.

She slammed the door shut from the outside.

He sat on one of the three armchairs and waited, not bothering to pick up one of the glossy magazines on the Pembroke table. A quarter of an hour became half an hour. Work had taught him to curb his impatience, but he was about to remind the battleaxe of his presence when he heard voices outside. He couldn't distinguish the words, but the rhythm of the speech suggested a man was asking for something and a woman – not the one who'd let him into the house – was refusing his request.

The speaking ceased and an outer door was shut. A moment later, Estelle entered. She was tall, dressed expensively and perfectly presented; not beautiful by sullen catwalk standards, she possessed the great advantage of quirkily attractive features touched with warm sensuality; when a man looked at her, he thought of bed. 'Miss Ryan?'

'Yes.'

She had a low-pitched voice with soft, velvet tones; when she whispered endearments, no doubt a man's mind spun. 'Detective Constable Metcalfe.'

'Maggie says you're not with the local force?' She crossed to the middle armchair and sat.

He could not remember previously having met a woman possessed of such discreet eroticism. 'As I told her, I'm with C Division.'

The door opened and Maggie looked in. 'You all right?'

'There's no problem,' Estelle answered.

'Have you made certain?'

'Not yet. There's no cause to worry.'

'I'll worry.' Maggie banged the door shut.

'Who's your detective inspector?' Estelle asked.

'Acton. It was Horner.'

'Who's the local Guv'nor?'

'Foley. And Woolley is the DS who took over from Blackey who got badly bust up in a car crash. I can carry on for a long time.'

'Maggie didn't believe you; said you were fake.'

213

'And I always thought I had an open, honest face.'

'Why are you here?'

'I think you may be able to help me.'

'How?'

'By answering a few questions.'

'About what?'

'Matters concerning the death of Detective Sergeant Frank Tobin.'

'Never met him.'

'There's no reason to believe you did.'

'Then?' She shrugged her shoulders.

Her breasts, as shapely as the Taj Mahal, had briefly jiggled. 'You know someone who's connected with the case.'

'And if I do?'

'You can provide the answers to those few questions.'

'It's unlikely.'

'You're acquainted with Simon Wyatt.'

'I've never met or even heard of him.'

'Like as not, he uses a different name when he comes here, but you'll have found out, one way or another, what his real one is. I've checked his phone accounts. He talks to you regularly. I want to learn why he made four calls to here, in very quick succession, on the tenth of March?'

'Did he?'

'I said.'

'I don't remember.'

'Concentrate.'

'Why should I?'

'When this case reaches court, everyone connected with it is going to be news. If his reason for phoning those four times is of no account to me, your name needn't appear.'

'How do I tell whether it is, or isn't, of account?'

'You don't, I do.'

'You're cocksure of yourself.'

'If I'm not, no one else will be.'

She leaned across to a small table, opened a chased silver cigarette box. 'Do you smoke?'

'I gave it up years ago, thanks all the same.'

'I wasn't offering, just curious.'

He laughed.

She lit the cigarette. 'I've a good friend who'll make your working life too tough to take if I tell him you've been threatening me.'

The chief constable? His salary might just be sufficient to pay for her pleasures – and his wife was reputed to be an ice maiden. 'I'm retired and brought back just for this one case. Your friend can shout all he likes and I'll give him the old two fingers.'

She let smoke drift out of her nostrils. 'Why are you asking about the phone calls?'

'I'm hoping what you tell me will explain Wyatt's state of mind when he arrived here.'

'I didn't know he'd kept phoning.'

'I thought we'd agreed to play our cards face upwards.'

'Maggie handles the calls.'

'Then find out what she can tell.'

She hesitated, then called out. 'Maggie.'

Maggie rushed into the room, making it clear she had been waiting outside. 'Giving trouble, is he?' she asked hoarsely, and perhaps hopefully.

'He's being a pet.'

Maggie made it clear she didn't like pets.

'Why did Tantalus phone four times one day back in March?'

'You're wanting me to tell the split?'

'That's right.'

Maggie looked as if she were about to spit, but contented herself with crossing her arms over her ample, shapeless bosom.

'Why did he phone four times?' Metcalfe asked.

'Because I first said she couldn't.'

'Couldn't what?'

Her nasal snort expressed contempt, sarcasm and disdain.

'Come on, Maggie,' Estelle said, 'lighten up.'

'Ain't it all so bleeding obvious a blind man could see it? He were desperate eager. I said you was busy and didn't have no free time, but he kept on and on until all I could do was work him in.'

As the price of a sweetener grew ever higher? 'Why was he so eager?' Metcalfe asked.

'Jesus! Even for a copper you ask dumb questions.'

'He didn't give any explanation in the hopes you'd be more helpful?'

'Just kept on and on as he had to be with her.'

Metcalfe briefly retired into thought. After a while, Maggie said, 'Is that it?'

'There's nothing more for the moment.'

She left, slamming the door even harder than before.

'Wyatt came here after the fourth phone call?' he said.

'Maybe.'

'Let's get more definite.'

'He turned up.' She stubbed out the cigarette.

'In what sort of mental state?'

'Eager.'

'Could you judge whether something unusual was firing him up?'

'He was nervous as well as eager; so nervous, things weren't OK.'

'What was his problem apart from the obvious one?'
'I don't know.'
'Come on, the more nervous, the more pillow talk.'
'Straight, all he said was something terrible had happened days before and he couldn't be certain how involved he was.'
'Those were his exact words?'
'Near enough.'
'Did he explain what he meant?'
'No.'
Here, surely, was evidence that Wyatt had been in Tobin's house that Tuesday night, but that he had not gone there with the intention of killing and so there was no premeditation; further, he had not been there when Tobin had hit his head on the table, collapsed, and died.
'I don't know what's the problem,' she said, breaking a long silence, 'but whatever it is, I'm telling you, he's a good man.'
'When he's been cheating on his wife?'
She spoke with sudden anger. 'You lot always find it easy to judge when you know bloody nothing.'
'Tell me what I don't know.'
'He won't screw his wife, however much he wants, because it will hurt her; always does since the daughter was born and the gynae man got impatient. How many men care what the woman thinks or feels? Tell me?'
'You're better able to answer than me.'
'The others who come here want extra to what they're getting, want to forget their pot bellies and bald heads; want to feel they're big by making it with someone much younger . . . He doesn't. Out of all the men, he's the only one who leaves contemptuous of himself, not of me.'
He said slowly: 'You make a good friend.'

'Don't believe me, do you? You lot never believe anyone.'

'You've told me a lot more truth than you can ever realize.' He stood.

'Where do I end in all this?'

He did not answer. When he left, Maggie was in the corridor, expression hostile, arms held as if ready for immediate action.

Twenty-Four

Metcalfe parked on the crest of a hill which over-looked the run of land down to the Channel. He stared through the windscreen at the patchwork of fields, hedges, and woods, at the villages and one town visible, at the sea which, as frequently happened, lacked a sharply defined horizon.

He was satisfied he could now confirm the course of events. Wyatt had faced Tobin. Tobin had prompted a scuffle, short-lived because he was too drunk to continue. Wyatt had left and called at his sister's where he had changed his torn shirt for one she'd had in the house. As would any good housewife, she had not thrown the collarless shirt away, but had kept it for rags. Faced with the possibility of being accused of causing Tobin's death and judging the ensuing distress this would bring his family, he had persuaded her to provide him with a false alibi. Wyatt's relationship with Estelle was a sign of strength, not weakness, of loyalty disloyally kept. His shock at Tobin's death and growing fear promoted by the criminal investigation had become so great he had had to find relief by visiting her, hence the four phone calls . . .

There could be no doubt what the law demanded – further investigation into Tobin's death. The consequences would be many. Although Wyatt – if believed – would

219

not be charged with murder or manslaughter, he and
Charlotte would be charged with conspiring to pervert
the course of justice; Wyatt's relationship with Estelle
would become public and Serena's total faith in his
loyalty would be shattered; Tobin, to the disgrace of
the whole county police force, would be publicly named
a criminal traitor and a drunken wife and child beater;
Victoria would be unable to continue to build a memory
of him that would hide the truth from herself and provide
her son with a father of whom to be proud; because
there were those reluctant to acknowledge anyone who,
however unknowingly, had been associated with guilt,
Roger Groves might bring to an abrupt end his growing
relationship with Victoria; Charlotte would have cause to
look back in time and bitterly understand how a certain
detective constable had, under the guise of friendship
and a growing love, surreptitiously questioned her to
determine her and her brother's guilt . . .

He gripped the steering wheel with a force that
whitened his knuckles. He'd always believed in an ideal
– justice was truth, truth was justice. But it seemed that
ideals were only for an idealistic world because in the real
world, truth could cause so much pain for the innocent as
well as the guilty that it was injustice.

He relaxed his grip on the steering wheel. At the bottom
of the hill, there was a T-junction – left to Setonhurst
and Detective Inspector Acton, right to Ronefield and
Charlotte. He started the engine and drove on. He would
turn right.